D0031524

Scenes from Early Life

Scenes from Early Life

Philip Hensher

ff

Faber and Faber, Inc.
An affiliate of Farrar, Straus and Giroux
New York

Faber and Faber, Inc.
An affiliate of Farrar, Straus and Giroux
18 West 18th Street, New York 10011

Copyright © 2012 by Philip Hensher
All rights reserved
Printed in the United States of America
Originally published in 2012 by Fourth Estate, Great Britain
Published in the United States by Faber and Faber, Inc.
First American edition, 2013

Library of Congress Cataloging-in-Publication Data
Hensher, Philip.
    Scenes from early life / Philip Hensher. — 1st American ed.
        p.   cm.
    "Originally published in 2012 by Fourth Estate, Great Britain" — T.p.
verso.
    ISBN 978-0-86547-761-2 (hardcover : alk. paper)
    1. Mahmood, Zaved, 1970– 2. Bangladesh—History—Revolution,
1971—Fiction. 3. India-Pakistan Conflict, 1971—Fiction. 1. Title.
PR6058.E554 S34 2012
823'914—dc23
                                                              2012022169

www.fsgbooks.com
www.twitter.com/fsgbooks · www.facebook.com/fsgbooks

1   3   5   7   9   10   8   6   4   2

For Richard Heaton

Contents

1: At Nana's House

1.

Even the shit of a dog smells good to you, if it's English.

(*Ingrazi kuttar gu-o tomar khache bhalo.*)

My grandmother used to say this to my grandfather. He was very pro-Empire. That was my mother's father, who used to call me Churchill when I cried. At first I did not know who Churchill was, but my grandfather would explain to me, and after a while I knew who he meant when he said Churchill. He meant me, and often he would ask to have me sit next to him at the lunch table. 'I want Churchill here,' he said, and I would be led up by my ayah, not crying at all. I felt very proud. The theory was that when Churchill was a little boy, he used to cry very much. All the time. He was a great reader of biographies, my grandfather.

When he went out to a friend's house, we would drive there in a big red car – a Vauxhall, I think. He was an income-tax lawyer, the president of the East Pakistan Income Tax Lawyers' Association. Later, the Bangla Desh Income Tax Lawyers' Association. There, at one old man's house or another, I would be allowed to stay in company for a while. He liked to show me off, and would call me Churchill in front of his friends. I don't believe that, as he said, he thought I would be the Churchill of Bangla Desh when I grew up. I think he mainly called me that because I cried.

My grandfather's great friend was called, by us, Mr Khandekar-nana. He had been a friend of my grandfather's from college, all the way back in the British time. They used to share a room when

1

they were at college, a long time ago in the 1930s, and ever afterwards, they were friends with each other. They had gone on being friends when they moved to Calcutta to be lawyers. (That was where they were in 1947.) And afterwards they had both moved to Dacca. My grandfather was Nana to us and his friend was Mr Khandekar-nana.

They both lived in the Dhanmondi area, very close to each other. It was the best place in Dacca to live. Nana's house was in road number six; Mr Khandekar-nana's was in road number forty. Both of them were two-storey houses with glass walls to the porch and flat roofs, both intricate and complex in their ground plan. It was only a ten-minute walk from Nana's house to Mr Khandekar-nana's, and it was a pleasant walk. The roads of Dhanmondi were quiet, and lined with trees, all painted white to four feet high, to discourage the ants. 'Ants can't walk on white,' my mother used to say. 'They are frightened of being seen. So that's why they paint the tree trunks white.' I still don't know how true that is. On the walk from Nana's house to Khandekar-nana's house, you would see only the occasional ayah, or mother, walking with her children, only the occasional houseboy loafing outside against the high, whitewashed walls of the houses, in those days. But my grandfather had a big red car, a Vauxhall, I think, and we drove the short distance to Mr Khandekar-nana's house.

Among the keen interests they shared were plants and flowers, and they kept their gardeners up to the mark. In front of their houses were roses, jasmine, dahlias, even sunflowers – English flowers, often. The two of them took pleasure in choosing flowers together, and their gardens were only different in small details. They were planted neatly, in rows, against the neat white Bauhaus style of their houses, and the mosaic in ash and white and green on the ground. The flowerbeds were in the sunniest part of the garden, away from the tamarind tree at the front of my grandfather's house, the mango tree at the front of Mr Khandekar-nana's.

The visits to Mr Khandekar-nana's followed the same sequence. My grandfather and Mr Khandekar-nana would go up to the balcony, shaded by the mango tree, and I would be allowed to go up with them. The tea would arrive and a plate of biscuits. My grandfather and Mr Khandekar-nana would take one biscuit each – one, one, judiciously, carefully, as lawyers do. Then I would be allowed to eat the rest. My grandfather would boast about how many books I had read, and as Khandekar-nana's wife arrived, to greet us and bring my grandfather up to date with her grand-children, he would mention that he thought in the end I would be the Churchill of Bangla Desh.

A great friend of mine was the daughter of another friend of my grandfather, a child specialist who lived quite opposite Nana's house. She was ten years older than I was. When we visited them, she would take me to her living room and feed me biscuits from her own tin. It had English pictures on top of it, of a house with hair for a roof and a pony eating from a lawn. She had a lot of books and a phonogram; still, it is the biscuits that I remember. I wonder now whether I was notorious in the neighbourhood. But I will explain why I was allowed to eat whatever I wanted when I come to it.

2.

He had a driver, my grandfather, which always very much impressed me. The driver's name was Rustum. Rustum stayed in the family for fifteen years, living with his family just next to the garage, outside the courtyard of the house. He was always very friendly to us children. I got to know him not because of our Sunday trips to my grandfather's friends, but because of what happened during the week. My grandmother would often ask Rustum to go to market for her. Rustum, too, liked me, and he would ask me and sometimes my sister to go with him. We always went because he slipped us a lozenge or a jujube at the end of the trip.

It was important that we would slip off with Rustum without mentioning it to anyone – the trip, like the secret jujube, was no fun if the grown-ups knew about it. But when I and my sister Sunchita were missed, my mother would start to shout and panic. My second aunty, Mary-aunty, would start to shout and panic. I know this because when we returned home, they would go on shouting and panicking at us, and at Rustum. 'Why couldn't you tell anyone that you were taking the children?'

We were kept under close surveillance, Sunchita and I, because we could never stay still. We were always chasing the chickens, climbing the mango tree in the garden, sneaking off to the market with Rustum, who conspired with us against the grown-ups. In the end, Rustum was sacked by my grandfather and died of tuberculosis.

3.

My grandfather and my grandmother fought a war of attrition over the balcony on the first floor. My grandfather thought it his possession, the place he could retreat to from the noise and crowd elsewhere. He had an image of his balcony as being like Mr Khandekar-nana's balcony and, I believe, thought of himself sitting on the cool open space, a cup of tea and biscuits to one side while the grandchildren and children, cousins and nephews and visitors from his village on business rampaged through the rest of the house.

There was a wooden armchair on the balcony, an orange-brown plantation chair with extendable limbs on which you could rest your legs. But it was generally pushed to one side, because my grandmother had her own ideas for the balcony. She encouraged the cook to see it as a useful space where things could be stored or placed to dry. Almost always, jolpai and mango were laid out there for drying, covered with dry spice on banana leaves; against the wall, rows of bottled pickles in mustard oil. It drove my grandfather mad with irritation that the balcony was being used in this way. 'This house is like a pickle factory,' he would mutter as, once again, he retreated from his balcony and went back downstairs to his library.

My challenge was to get on to the balcony while my grandmother was busy with other things. The tamarind tree was old, and thick-leaved; its boughs thrust beneath the roof and into the balcony's space. If nobody was about, I climbed the tree and dropped softly on to the balcony. Or sometimes my sister Sunchita and I would conceal ourselves behind a curtain, or underneath a table, waiting for the servants to go by, and then we would run up to my grandfather's room, and afterwards on to the balcony.

There, we hid. I liked to taste the pickles that had been laid out; I liked the pucker they made on my tongue.

4.

We did not live at my grandfather's house, but we went there for the weekend, almost every weekend. We especially went there if there was a good movie on television. We knew that there was a movie on television every Sunday afternoon and Saturday evening. It was often a Calcutta movie, an old Satyajit Ray film or something of that sort. Still, my father refused to buy a television for us, and so we went eagerly to Nana's house.

The television was placed in the dining room, at the end of the polished mahogany table, which could seat, and often did seat, twelve people. Only Grandfather and Grandmother, Nana and Nani, had their own allotted places.

As well as having no television, my parents had, at that time, no car. We would arrive in a rickshaw at lunchtime on Friday – a cycle-rickshaw, with room for four. There was always a fight between me and the younger of my two sisters, Sunchita, over who would get to sit on my mother's lap. My elder sister was above such things, and my big brother, Zahid, too. He was aloof, and came when he chose.

At lunch on Friday there would be guests from my grandfather's village, his cousins or sisters, on a journey to Dacca for purposes of their own. The faces came and went. There would be hilsha fish, rice, some of the cook's pickles, such as a mango pickle from the mango tree at the back of the garden, or jolpai. Jolpai is a small sour berry, about the size of an olive. My grandmother, with her sharp tongue, ruled over the lunch table on Friday. It was a time for children and for the women, of whom there were many in our family.

After lunch, we children went to bed. At night we slept downstairs, but in the afternoon we were put to bed in an aunt's room, upstairs. It was Mary-aunty's job to get us to bed, and she shouted at us: 'Go to bed – take a book.' But we did not rest. My sister Sunchita and I would spend the time fighting. We always wanted to read the same book, though Sunchita was a better reader than I was. I liked books with pictures in them; Sunchita read a novel by Sharat Chandra Chattapadhaya when she was only eight, a novel for adults. ('Why are you reading this book? This book is not for you,' my grandfather said, surprised but not angry.) In the hour of rest, I would demand that Sunchita read her book out to me, or if I was crotchety, that she give it to me. And so we fought.

My grandfather came home from his lawyer's chambers at five, or half past five. The creak and gong-like echo of the opening gate; then his red car, a Vauxhall, driven by Rustum, with its engine noise unlike any other engine noise; and then my grand-father's voice downstairs. 'Is anyone here?' he said, his voice hardly above conversation pitch. But, of course, there was always somebody there. It was a game between him and me. Of all the people in the house, I called, 'Nana, I am here.'

Then he would say, 'Churchill! You are here. When did you arrive?' That was the signal to get up and go to greet my grand-father.

My grandfather was a very competitive person, and once he had changed out of his Western suit into what he liked to wear in the evening, a white Panjabi and white pyjamas, he might tease my mother with stories of what my father, his son-in-law, had got up to during the day. As my father and my grandfather were both lawyers in the same field of income-tax law, they sometimes found themselves on opposite sides of a case. My grandfather never let this opportunity fall.

'Mahmood tried to be very intelligent today,' he would say, waiting for the tea, biscuits and nuts – he was very fond of nuts – to arrive. 'But it all fell very flat.'

'Which case was that?' my mother asked. Before she married, she, too, had started to train as a lawyer; she still helped out with legal research. She liked to talk about the law with my father, and her father, too. My grandfather explained, going into detail. 'I'm sure he made a very good case,' my mother said loyally.

'Mahmood tried to be very intelligent today,' my grandfather said, laughing, 'but it didn't succeed at all.'

7

5.

These are the names of the aunts who came to dinner at Nana's house almost every Friday night.

Mira-aunty had moved to Canada, so she did not come.

Nadira-aunty was in England, in Sheffield, with her husband.

And Boro-mama, Big-uncle, the eldest of Nana's children, had his own house in Dacca and his own family, so he did not come, although he had left one of his sons behind with Nana and Nani, as if absent-mindedly.

Those aunts and that uncle did not come for dinner.

But Nana sat at the head of the table, and to his left sat Nani, my grandmother. She had a highly polished teak stool for her leg to rest on; it had a long hollow on it, which I used to imagine had been worn away by her leg, over hundreds, thousands, of family dinners. But I think it was really made that way. From time to time she would call for a servant to give her a massage in the middle of dinner.

My grandmother loved to talk about food, though for her the best food was always food she had eaten in the past, and not the food she had just eaten. She allowed a certain amount of time to pass – years, usually – before she would award a compliment. The only daughter who loved food as much as she did was Bubbly, and they could keep up conversations about individual long-ago dishes for hours. Bubbly could remember, in quite specific detail, the dishes her sisters had had at their weddings, and she and her mother would happily go over them, or food they had eaten at other times.

'Do you remember?' Nani would say, her leg resting on the teak footrest. 'Do you remember the steamed rui that Sharmin taught Ahmed how to make when everyone was living here? Do you remember, Bubbly? It was so good, that steamed rui with lemon and ginger. And she taught him, and he never got it right afterwards. I don't know why. But it was never so delicious ever again. He didn't listen properly, or he made some changes of his own, wretched boy, and completely spoiled the dish. Oh, I loved to eat that steamed rui. I could have eaten it every day.'

'It was so clever of her,' Dahlia would say, calling from half a table away. 'It is so strange that it was her to be so clever with fish, being Bihari, and not liking fish as much as we do.'

'Well, Dahlia,' Nani said. 'She didn't like fish at the beginning. But she came to like it because your big brother likes it so much. And now she likes it as much as anyone, and she has such clever ways with it.'

'Because, of course,' Bubbly said, taking no notice of her mother, 'there was not always a great choice of things to eat, that year, but you could often get rui when there was no other fish to be had. I wish Sharmin would come back and teach Ahmed how to make it again, but she says she can't remember, and she says she doesn't know what's wrong with the way Ahmed cooks it, so that would really be a fool's errand.'

Nani and Nana had the best view of the television, which was at the far end of the table, on the sideboard next to a little fridge for all sorts of odds and ends. Dinner took place at eight, because that was when the television news was on.

Next to my grandmother sat Mary-aunty. She was the eldest of the sisters, after my mother. It was her job to keep the children under control, but she could often be tearful when faced with determined opposition, and I wonder if she was very good at her household task.

Next to her sat Shibli, who was Boro-mama's son. I was very jealous of Shibli. Whereas we only came to visit Nani and Nana at weekends, Shibli lived with them all the time, and visited Boro-mama, his father, only occasionally. This seemed to me the height of glamour, and it made me sick to see the ways in which Shibli was spoilt by my grandparents.

Choto-mama, Little-uncle, came next. His name was Pultoo. He was not much older than the bigger children, and was still at college. He was not a lawyer; he was an artist. In an odd way, my grandfather was rather proud of that: he used to say, 'If Pultoo wants to, he wants to.' Some people assumed that Choto-mama had to sit next to Shibli, with his spoilt ways, as a punishment from my grandfather. But that was not true: my grandfather had given Pultoo a large room with sunny windows on the ground floor of his house as a studio. He was rather proud of him, as I say.

Then his sister, Bubbly-aunty, the youngest of my aunts, and then Sunchita and Sushmita, my sisters. They sat at the end of the table, next to the television, which they could not see very well, and the fridge, which they often had to open and fetch something from for my grandfather.

The far end of the table was not a good place to sit, and there might be placed a village aunt or uncle, a cousin travelling to Dacca on business. And next to them, working back on the other side of the table, might be Dahlia-aunty, my favourite, and Era-aunty. And I was between them and my mother. My grandfather called me Churchill; the rest of the family called me Saadi. Dahlia would lean over and encourage me to eat, especially delicious little things; she would talk to me about pickles in her memory. Nadira I loved, because she was such a good singer, though, of course, not at the dinner table. And my mother sat by my grandfather, as the eldest daughter.

Two uncles, Boro-mama and Choto-mama, Big-uncle and Little-uncle; six aunts, Mary, Era, Mira, Nadira, Dahlia, Bubbly. Dahlia was my favourite and I was hers.

6.

Once, Pultoo-uncle was late for dinner. He was expected, but had gone out in the afternoon and had not returned by the time my grandfather came back. Pultoo had a wide circle of friends at the college of art, and occasionally he was seen in a café or ambling through a park, gesticulating and talking in the middle of ten friends. He was the only one in the family to wear traditional dress all the time, a long shirt and pyjama trousers. The rest of the family were proud of him, and thought that he could dress as he chose. He was thin and dark, with hair that swept back like a film star's and big eyes set deep in his face. When he was excited, as, in conversation, he often was, his hands chopped the air, like a cook's at work.

It was understood that Pultoo-uncle had gone out to a class at the college of art that morning. My sister Sunchita and I had been allowed to watch the television in the dining room. We had seen *Double Deckers*, and *Tom and Jerry*, and a new programme made in Bangladesh. My sister, who liked to lie on her stomach on the dining-table when she watched television, had been shooed off when the table was set; the children's programmes had come to an end, and the adults' programmes begun. Soon it would be the news and dinnertime. About the house there was the sense that the kitchen was ready and waiting, the dishes now being kept warm. My grandfather was not a stickler about mealtimes, but he liked to know if someone was going to be late.

'I hope nothing is wrong,' Mary-aunty said.

'Wrong?' Era said, alarmed.

'Nonsense, nothing could be wrong,' Dahlia-aunty said, although everyone remembered the time, not so long before, when young men had failed to come home and were never seen again. That possibility lingered for many years, and people did their families the kindness of being punctual, on the whole, to save their nerves.

But Pultoo-uncle came in, as the clock in the hall struck eight, brushing his hair back with his hand and depositing a table-top-sized folder by the front door, apologizing as he came. Warm, he smelt of geraniums, and his long shirt was dusty with the red dust of the street. He had two friends with him, two other artists. Their names were Kajol and Kanaq. Kanaq fascinated me and my sisters because she came from a tribe; her appearance was highly

11

exotic, with her slanted eyes and sleepy air. It was not unusual for Pultoo to bring friends for dinner, and these two often arrived at my grandfather's house in the late afternoon on a Friday, and stayed for dinner with only a little urging, only one diffident invitation. They lived in lodgings, and I believe they enjoyed the chance of a family dinner. My grandfather did not really care who came for dinner; my grandmother, on the other hand, liked to be given the chance to offer an invitation.

'Can we find space for these two?' Pultoo said, when he came back from washing, his face wet and glistening, his white teeth shining. 'I'm sure there is space.'

My grandmother muttered something, and went off to the kitchen with the bare appearance of graciousness.

'I do like them,' my sister Sunchita said, in her adult, mature, book-reading way about the guests, as we went back to the dining room to catch the rest of the television before the news started. 'But their painting is awful.'

7.

When the news was finished, my grandmother asked Pultoo what he had been doing at the art college that morning. He asked her permission to get out the drawings from his life class, which he had left in the folder. He passed them round the table; they were charcoal drawings of a naked man sitting on a box. 'I think this one is the best,' my grandfather said simply, when they got to him.

'And we were late because we were planning something,' Pultoo said.

'Yes,' Mary-aunty said. 'You certainly were late.'

'Late, yes,' Era said. She often agreed with her sisters, in an echo; she was shy and did not venture her own opinions easily. Even her echoes of opinions were often given first in the direction of her plate.

'We really got carried away,' Kanaq said, her slanting eyes looking at the biriani. 'It is such a good idea.'

'We are going to produce greetings cards,' Kajol said. 'People always like greetings cards – we are going to give them something special.'

My uncle went on to explain that their plan was for hand-made cards, sketches in pen and ink, in watercolours and in pencil, and to sell them on a stall in Ramana field in the first instance. 'After that, if it is successful, we can think about opening a shop,' Pultoo said. 'It is such a good idea, I don't know why no one has thought of it before.'

The cards would be for the new year. In Bangladesh, Choto-mama said, people were always sending cards for any reason; but they were mass-produced, the same cards that were sold anywhere, and did not speak to the sender or to the recipient. 'I saw a birthday card,' my uncle's friend Kajol said. 'It was a photograph of a mountainside in the Himalaya, I expect, and the message inside was "This is what I dream of . . ." It means nothing, that kind of thing. Produced in factories, designed by slaves.'

'Yes,' Pultoo said, in his excitable way. 'People would not buy that if they could buy the sort of thing we are going to make for them.'

'What sort of thing?' my grandmother said.

I wondered whether their idea was to make cards with pictures of naked people on them. I did not think people would want to buy those. But Pultoo-uncle explained that they would be drawing and painting famous views in Bangladesh, typical scenes of Bangladesh, such as a village house or a tea plantation, perhaps even well-known corners of Dacca. 'I would much prefer to see a hand-drawn picture like that,' Pultoo said.

'When are your teachers coming?' Shibli called to Dahlia-aunty. 'The musicians.'

'Quiet, Shibli,' Nani said, in her stagy way. 'Don't you have any respect? Your uncle is talking about your country.'

'Your country, yes,' Era said.

13

8.

The servants in my grandfather's house held a fascination for me. I never knew how many there were. After Mary-aunty had put my sister and me to bed in the afternoons, we would often start up a row, a pillow fight, a shouting match, and soon she would come to see what the noise was. But she was somebody who could not pass another human being known to her in any degree without greeting them. So we could hear the passage of Mary-aunty through the house from her slapping chappals, and from a constant stream of greetings, and expressions of concern and interest: 'Good afternoon, Rustum'; 'How are your children, Timur; is your daughter happy with Mr Khandekar . . .' That sort of thing. There were enough servants to slow her progress, to warn us and allow us to calm down and pretend to be asleep by the time she opened the door to shout at us.

My grandfather had a gardener called Atish. Over the years, he had become both an inside servant and an outside servant, according to need. I was not allowed to follow Atish about when he was inside, cleaning and polishing. When he was gardening, there were no objections to my walking about with him and asking him any number of questions. There was plenty to occupy him: the huge bougainvillaeas that poured out of pots and formed a blazing arch, the way that the terrace and entrance needed to be swept of dead leaves and flowers. He trimmed back the flowers in the flowerbeds; he carried out mysterious surgical operations with saw and secateurs on the fruit trees – the guava tree, the mango tree, the jackfruit tree, the banana tree, the tamarind tree, with its neatly diagrammatic leaves and its extravagant flower. There was plenty of digging and pruning and planting to do, with a small boy gazing and a chicken or two following round in the hope of an upturned worm.

Atish was a poor Hindu who was left behind in 1947. Grandfather and Grandmother had had to leave Calcutta in a great hurry and come to Dacca. Nana had bought a house in Rankin Street from a rich Hindu, who had had to leave Dacca in a great hurry and go to Calcutta. I wondered why they had not simply swapped their houses, but they had not. Atish had not gone like the rich Hindus to Calcutta: he had stayed where he was, and Grandfather had taken pity on him and employed him in the garden. It suited him.

Nana liked to employ poor and vulnerable people. All of them stayed for ever. And Nana's relations with them sometimes surprised his friends, since he encouraged the people he employed to speak their minds to him. Sometimes they developed independent habits, which could prove inconvenient to the rest of the household. Rustum, Nana's driver, was another of these vulnerable people, but after a while, he developed the habit of taking the car out on his own, or of ignoring instructions. Sometimes my grandmother would come out after lunch, expecting Rustum to be there to drive her to a friend's house, and would find that he had gone out with the car, and no one knew where he had gone. When he came back, I had heard him blame Dahlia-aunty, saying that she had told him to go and fetch something from a shop on the other side of Dacca. She had demanded, he would say, a particular sort of sandesh, one that could only be got in a confectioner's shop on Sadarghat. He knew the sort of blame that could be convincingly put on Dahlia. But if this got back to Dahlia-aunty, she would fly into a furious passion. It was the first thing that came into Rustum's mind, it seemed, and it did not occur to him that anyone might ask Dahlia whether there was any truth in his story.

'How could he? How could he? How could he?' Dahlia would shout, sometimes audibly from outside the gates of the house. To passers-by and neighbours, it did not seem obvious that these screams were caused only by a servant's unreliable events; surely, they must have thought, a husband or father must have threatened a beating to the victim, at the very least. But nobody beat anyone in Nana's house, and Dahlia screamed because Rustum had pretended she had ordered him about.

Finally there came the terrible day when Rustum had a fight with Nana himself. It occurred in the week. When we arrived that Friday, Rustum was not there. This was not unusual, but it was strange that the red Vauxhall was in the garage when both Nana and Rustum were out of the house. When Nana came home, he came home in a cycle-rickshaw, and I understood that something atrocious had happened. Rustum had been asked to leave. 'I could forgive him for taking the car without permission,' my grandfather said, a week or two later when he could bring himself to talk about it. 'But it was the lying afterwards I could not put up with.' My grandfather, however, immediately felt guilty about evicting Rustum and his family from the flat in the servants' block, and made it his business to find Rustum another place to live and even another job. When, five years later, Rustum was diagnosed with tuberculosis, my grandfather paid for his treatment.

Atish the gardener was not as popular with the children as Rustum. He did not have the glamour of a red Vauxhall car to carry out his trade, but only a spade, a hoe, a trowel and a fork; among his tools, only the secateurs, with their terrible grip and savage slice, had the power to fascinate. But I liked to follow him around the garden, and watch him at his tasks, and he did not object. Sometimes he let me undertake a small task to help him, such as filling his two watering-cans. If it was cold, Atish used to wear a shawl about his shoulders, a scarf wound right around his head, like a sufferer from the toothache; his set face emerged from a kind of red cotton nest on the coldest days of the year.

Atish would start work at the front of the house, where the tamarind tree shaded the entrance. There were always things to sweep up here. Then he would move on to the flowerbeds at the side of the house in the full sun, and then to the back of the house, with the other fruit trees, the lawn and, underneath the jackfruit tree, the chicken house. The chickens were allowed to wander the garden, eating whatever they could find. One of the days that Atish devoted to digging and turning over the earth in the flowerbeds was a festival day for the chickens, as they could eye and pounce on a worm or a beetle that Atish's spade had uncovered. They stood, beadily eyeing his work, like supervisors in a factory.

The chicken house had been made and painted, decorated, by Choto-mama Pultoo. He had started it when he was still at school and showing signs of artistic and practical talent. He had painted a frame, put a tidy little net in its front, and then, he said, he had wondered what he would like in his house, if he were a chicken. So the chicken house contained the dead branches of trees for the chickens to perch on, and the back wall had a landscape painted by Pultoo. 'So that they can think of the wide open spaces of the countryside, even when they are confined in a small garden in Dacca,' Pultoo poetically observed. The chickens seemed to take more pleasure in the dead tree, on which they happily roosted and slept, than in the landscape, which they ignored. Within a few months, the mountain view was dimmed and smeared by chicken feathers and chicken shit. Pultoo was not put off, and carried on adding ornament and furniture to the chicken house in the hope of broadening their mental horizons. The latest was a series of terracotta yogurt pots, which he had decorated with some folk-like paintings of milkmaids.

'Come on,' Dahlia-aunty, who was a good sort, would sometimes say to me when we arrived at my grandfather's house for the weekend. 'Let's go and see what Choto-mama has done to the chicken run this week.'

Atish never made any comment on Pultoo's chicken run, or on the chickens themselves for that matter. He stayed silent on the subject, even when the cat next door got into the garden and killed three chicks. He ignored the chickens standing by his side, watching him hoe and dig, though he would pause in his regular rhythm if they darted forward to grab a worm.

I could stand there all morning, watching Atish work and the chickens eat the grubs he found for them. The only things he said to me were odd horticultural pieces of advice: it was necessary to

17

prune a mango tree in March; the first sprouts from seeds that would turn into sunflowers must be thinned out when they had reached an inch tall; you could not water a bougainvillaea enough. It was as if he thought I was going to become a gardener like him when I grew up. The way he gave horticultural maxims is clear in my head, but not what he said exactly. I may have got them quite wrong. But I stood or squatted there all morning, watching Atish at work, watching the white chickens dart to and fro.

9.

My father came before lunch on Saturday. He did not come with a dramatic flourish, like my grandfather; he did not come with excitement, like my mother and my sisters. He came under a pile of papers, tied up with red ribbon, and in a pernickety, unenthusiastic way. Sometimes he was carrying so much that it threatened to overbalance him. It is not easy to travel with a large bundle of papers in the back of a cycle-rickshaw, and he often turned up with his arms in a desperate position, clutching them like a large escaping fish. I liked to watch him arrive. The cycle-rickshaw he always used was glittering silver, polished, with the faces of film stars under a setting sun painted on the back of its canopy; like many of the other rickshaws of Dacca, its canopy was lined with tinsel, like a fur-lined hood. The rickshaw driver, however, was a taciturn, serious man, whom you could not imagine decorating his vehicle in this way, and so was my father, sitting in the square middle of the rickshaw with his papers on his lap, his lawyer's white bands around his throat.

Both I and my father were hypocrites – he, because he did not really want to come to my grandfather's house: he was a government lawyer, my grandfather was a lawyer for the people, so they were always on opposite sides, and my grandfather could never resist needling him about this argument or other that he had

18

undertaken with less success than he had hoped for. He came because he felt he ought to, and because the Bar library in which he did so much of his work closed at weekends.

I was a hypocrite because, towards the end of Saturday morning, I made a habit of going up to Nana's balcony to watch out for Father's arrival. The balcony had by far the best view down the street, and it was where anyone sat to keep an eye out for an eagerly awaited visitor. From there, you could see the curious events of the street: a handcart laden with megaphones, like silver tropical flowers, heading to a rally, or a pitiful hawker, selling a single useless part of a household object, such as the handles of a pressure cooker, laid out on a cloth in the forlorn hope of a purchaser. I went up there, making sure that everyone knew I was going up there, to watch out for Father's arrival in a cycle-rickshaw. In fact, my father's arrival was nothing to look forward to. I disliked the way my mother and aunts had less time for me, busy with meeting his needs. He was much more remote than my aunts and my mother, and the idea of creating fun for his children would not have occurred to him. I made a great performance out of my anticipation because I thought that was the right, or the dramatic, thing to do. But in fact I did not much care that I had not seen him since early breakfast on Friday, and would not have minded if I had not seen him until Monday morning. Like many little boys, I wanted to have my mother to myself, with her warm iron-scented flesh, her ripple of silk against my face when she embraced me.

The one thing that made the weekend visits to Nana endurable for my father was that Nana had an excellent law library of his own. Although the public law library was closed at weekends, my father could, once he had eaten lunch with the aunts, his parents-in-law and the children, retreat to Nana's library and carry on working in its rusty warm light. Sometimes he would call Sunchita and me in, and set us the task to find a particular book in Nana's library, or a particular case within a book. I believe he thought he was providing us with some fun, as well as with a little education.

19

The library had a double aspect: one barred window looked out to the tamarind tree at the front, the other at the flowerbed to the side. Out of the front window, I could see the watchman leaning on the bonnet of the red Vauxhall. The big front gate of the house was open, and he was talking to someone I could not see. From the side window, there was Atish, attending to the flowerbeds. There was no one to fill his watering-cans for him, and he was trudging backwards and forwards with an uncomplaining uneven gait, like a badly oiled clockwork toy that threatened to start walking in circles. 'Liberty Cinema versus CIT,' my father said, in his light-toned voice. 'Have you found that one for me?'

Elsewhere in the house the television was on, and Shibli was watching; Mary-aunty's slapping chappals were coming down the stairs, and she was greeting the cook by asking about her daughter. My grandfather was laughing somewhere. Behind everything, the quiet of the Dhanmondi street, and the peaceful burble of the chickens in the garden.

2: The Game of *Roots*

1.

The children all around watched American television shows with absorption, and would not be distracted. They watched *Knight Rider* and *Kojak*, *Dallas* and *Starsky and Hutch*, and other things still less suitable for small children. Afterwards, they rushed out into the street, into each other's gardens and homes, dizzy and full of games of re-enactment. For weeks after Starsky and Hutch had rescued a girl bound and imprisoned in a church crypt, nurses, ayahs, mothers and aunts kept discovering small girls in their charge tied up with washing line to jackfruit trees. They had been abandoned in the joy of the game and, unable to untie themselves, wailed until someone rescued them.

'Little brutes,' Dahlia-aunty would say, when Sunchita, Shibli and I roared in after a morning playing some delirious game, wild-haired and dirty. 'Go and wash yourselves immediately.'

'Immediately,' Era would add.

The games were played in the street, in gardens, on any spare plot of ground, with fervour and without planning. When we came across a neighbour's children or grandchildren, we would start a game of *Starsky and Hutch* without any discussion. We knew all the children for many houses around, all the short-cuts between gardens, and the houses we would be chased away from.

In the streets, we lost all our respectability, and became, as our aunts told us, little ragamuffins. Sometimes, in our racing about, we got as far as Mirpur Road, where we were forbidden to go on our own. It was exciting there: the streets were suddenly full of trades. You could see the aubergine-seller, frying white discs in his yellow oil, the black iron cauldron precariously balanced on the gas stove; the cracker of nuts; a pavement cobbler; the barber with his cut-throat razor attending to a man leaning back in a chair under a tree, a broken scrap of mirror all he had to work with to perfect the moustache. There was the chai-wallah with his little terracotta cups, waiting to be filled with tea, and a hundred potsherds lying around him from the morning's custom. We raced around all of them, playing our TV games, further than we ever meant to go, ignoring their curses and delirious in our rule-breaking. We all knew that Mirpur Road was where a little boy had been kidnapped and eaten by starving people, and we ran through its chaos and indifference, yelling like urchins.

We played *Kojak* and *Knight Rider* and *Double Deckers* constantly, without much preference for one game over another. Perhaps there was not much difference between the games. *Dallas* was more of a girl's game. My sisters never got tired of parading up and down the garden and pointing a vengeful finger at the small girl from Mrs Rahman's house. 'Ten million dollars!' they would cry. The rest of us were happy pretending to be talking cars, being kidnappers, or trying to walk like Hungry Bear.

The hold these television programmes had over our imaginations was swept away in one moment by a new series. My aunts talked about it seriously some time before it even started. The whole world, they said, had watched this series, and now it was coming to us, to be shown on Bangladesh television. It was the first time I realized that the programmes we watched were not made especially for us, although most of the television we watched was about people who did not look at all like us.

The programme was called *Roots*, and was about a family of black people. They started by living in Africa, then were kidnapped and taken to America, where they were slaves. We were entranced. It did not seem to agree with our idea of America at all. The next day we lifted the bolt, pushed the iron gates open and ran out

22

across the street, not troubling to close the gates behind us. For once, we did not mooch or loiter until we came across some children we knew. We banged on doors like drunkards, demanding that our playfellows came out. 'Did you see *Roots*?' we shouted, and everyone had. Finally, there were twenty children, all nearly overcome with excitement, spilling across the quiet street under the trees and shouting their heads off.

'I want to be Kunta Kinte,' one said.

'No, I want to be,' another said. And my sister said she would be Kunta Kinte's wife. Shibli was a brother who was to be killed. He liked to be killed in games, so long as he could stand up straight away and go to be killed all over again.

'So I'm walking down the riverbank with my wife,' Kunta Kinte said, balancing along the gutter. 'Oh, wife, wife, I love you so much.'

'Oh, husband,' Sunchita said. A fight was breaking out between the slave-traders and the Africans. 'Stop it, stop it, you've got to watch me. Look, watch me, I'm walking with my husband Kunta Kinte.'

Shibli got up from being killed. 'Who's the chief slave-owner? I want to be the chief slave-owner.'

'You can't be,' a boy called Assad shouted. 'You don't know how to kill anyone. I want to be the chief slave-owner. I want to come and put Kunta Kinte in chains and steal him to America.'

'You don't know how to kill anyone either,' Sunchita said to Assad. He was a boy we only sometimes saw. We had not called at his house, three houses away; he had heard the noise and the shouts of '*Roots*' and had come out of his own accord. 'You can't be the chief slave-owner.'

'I know how people are killed,' Assad said. 'It's not fair.'

I was clamouring like all the others to be allowed to be the chief slave-owner, the Englishman. That was the thing I wanted to be. And then a miracle happened. Kunta Kinte intervened and said, with calm authority, 'Saadi should be the slave-owner. After all, he's the palest among us. He can be the white man.' And that was that, and I was the slave-owner, because, after all, Kunta Kinte was the hero of the game and what he said went.

Assad rushed at me with both fists flying. I hated to fight – when I fought with my sisters, it was always in play. I had never done anything worse to anyone than throw an orange directly at Sunchita's head. I dodged behind my big sister Sushmita, who had no such reluctance. She pushed him, hard, and he fell over in the dust, wailing.

'I don't want to play this game,' Assad howled. But he did not run away. The game was too good for that. In ten minutes' time, he was lining up gleefully with all the other slaves behind Kunta Kinte and his wife, while I growled, 'This is my slave ship, and you are all under my power for ever and ever.' One of my two assistant slave-keeping Englishmen had got the plum role of the man with the whip – a torn-off vine – and he now dramatically brought it down on the backs of the ten slaves, hunched and moaning. Two small girls of the neighbourhood, the daughters of Mr Khandekar-nana's niece, were happily screaming for help. They were tied with washing line to the roadside trees. Over the road, a houseboy was watching with fascination, perhaps wanting to abandon his duties and come over to join in. It was the best game we ever played, and we played it every Sunday afternoon for many weeks.

2.

Whenever a chick emerged from Pultoo-uncle's chicken house, my sisters, Shibli and I would rush to see it. We would have warning. A mother hen would sit on her eggs inside the chicken house, blowing her feathers out into a big angry ball and clucking. And then one morning there would be some small puffs of yellowish feathers with the big feet of a toy, and eyes with a strange, tired, aged look. My sisters made small girlish piping noises to echo the little squeaks; Shibli would always pick one up, sometimes making the mother hen rush at him with her neck outstretched. The hens were so sharp and businesslike, getting on with their occupations, but their chicks were fluffy and yellow and not like animals at all, but like things run by inner machinery. I did not torment them, but liked to watch them, dipping their heads into the waterbowl left for them by Atish the gardener, running back to their mothers, making their small cries for attention. I could sit on my haunches, watching them, for hours.

Once, I was alone in the garden watching some day-old chicks in this way, quite silently. The others were inside – Sushmita was reading, Shibli was making a nuisance of himself in the kitchen, and Sunchita had been sent to bed in disgrace. I had seen chicks hatch from their eggs; the struggle inside the shell was hateful to me – I always feared that the effort would be too much for them. And when they emerged, they were so wet and slimy, so ugly, I could not help imagining how frightening they would be, with their sudden sharp gestures, if they were the same size as me.

But within hours they were small and round and fluffed quite yellow, and seemed nearly at home in the world. They stretched their plump little wings, like stubby fingers, and, not able to fly, fell from the chicken house on to the lawn under the jackfruit tree. Their movements were undecided and sudden, and you could not know what would cause them to take fright, or when they would move confidently.

'They're born standing,' Atish the gardener said. He had laid down his tools and was now standing behind me. I think he liked watching the newly hatched chicks as much as I did. 'Not like human beings. Human beings can't feed themselves, they can't walk, not for years. A chicken makes his own way out of the shell, punches his way out, and then he cleans himself off, and he stands on his two feet and off he goes like you or me. First thing he does is to find something to eat, and it's the same food he'll eat all his life.'

This was true. I watched the chicks pecking at the seeds on

the ground. It was exactly what the fully grown chickens ate. From the house came the sound of music: Dahlia-aunty was having a music lesson, with tabla and harmonium, and her lovely singing voice filled the garden.

'Can I have a chick of my own?' I asked Atish.

'It's not for me to say,' Atish said.

But he reached into the pocket of his grimy shirt and took out a chapatti. It might have been there for him to eat later, or it might have been in his shirt for some time. He tore off a corner and gave it to me. 'If you get a chick to come to you,' he said, 'it will be your friend.'

I took it, and held it out on the palm of my hand. I had the attention of the chicks. I lowered my hand almost to the ground. After a moment, a chick detached itself from the others, and came up, quite boldly, investigating. He pecked swiftly at the corner of the chapatti in the palm of my hand. He was not committing himself, staying in a place he could run from if I turned out to be an enemy, tempting him into a trap. I wondered at the cunning of a creature so small and so young in days. But then, as I did not move, but just let him go on pecking at the corner of Atish's chapatti, he made some kind of decision, and hopped up on to the palm of my hand, where he could get at the bread more comfortably. He was darker than the other chicks, almost brown in hue, with two parallel black squiggles along his back, running along where his wings were.

'You see?' Atish said. 'That one likes you. He'll always remember you, now.'

'How can he remember?' I said.

'I don't know,' Atish said. He threw his shawl over his shoulder, picked up his fork again. 'But he always will. Sometimes when they come up to you, they think that you're their mother, and then they never change their mind.'

The idea that my chick thought I was his mother was so funny that I trembled with laughter. The chick jumped off my hand, but did not run away; he went on pecking nonchalantly around my hand as if the movement of my laughter had been an

26

inexplicable quake. And in a moment he returned to me, and hopped back on my palm.

When I went back into the house, I told everyone that I had a chicken all of my own and had decided to call him Piklu. My sisters, Mary-aunty and Bubbly-aunty, who had come from Srimongol to visit, all came out to see my chicken. 'Don't go too close,' Mary-aunty warned. 'You'll upset the mother and she might even eat her own chicks.' But I knew that would not happen, unless my sisters and aunts came running across and crowded them. I approached the mass of new chicks pecking at the ground before the chicken house, walking softly, and what happened did not surprise me at all. The chick with the two black squiggles down its back, the one a little darker than the others, detached itself quite easily from its brothers and sisters and came to say hello to me. I squatted down, and held out my hand, and the chick hopped happily on to my palm.

'This is Piklu,' I said. 'He's my chicken.'

And Bubbly-aunty was so impressed, she went to fetch Dahlia out of her music lesson to show her.

3.

Every aunt had her occupation – to paint, to cook, to help Nana with legal research, to attend to the chickens. Bubbly, who loved food, was forever in the kitchen, though her particular task was to supervise the making of the pickles. Mary's was to keep the children in order; Nadira's was to sing. Though she was in Shef-field now, the other aunts talked about her ceaselessly. I could remember her wedding, how beautiful it had been, how beautiful she had been. Her singing had been good enough for her to appear on Bangladeshi television, performing Tagore songs. 'Do you think she has her own programme, by now, on British television?' Mary asked guilelessly.

'I wouldn't be at all surprised,' Nani said.

At the time when Tagore was banned by the Pakistanis, before independence, Nadira had hidden her music with all the other Bengali music, poetry and books in the secret cellar at my grandfather's house. When it was safe to bring it out again, it was clear that she had not forgotten any of it. That was her occupation.

Dahlia was my favourite aunt. Nadira had been fascinating and dramatic, always ready to shout and stamp or even to cry for effect in public. But she could also say, 'Be off with you, wretched child.' Dahlia was as fragrant as Nadira had been, and as pretty as her name. She, too, had her music. It was understood that Nadira was a better singer, but Dahlia took lessons from the two musicians who came to the house. Her occupation, however, since Nadira had taken music as her first choice, was to sew: she embroidered very deft, very intricate scenes of country life, not using patterns, but quite out of her head. If you asked her, she would explain that this figure was a man she had seen working in the fields near my grandfather's village last summer, that this was his wife, waiting for him at home and cooking a delicious supper, that these were what she imagined his children looked like, and these were the mountains in the distance, with cows and goats on them. Pultoo was very scathing about Dahlia's sewing and her designs, but many people loved them, and she was always being asked for her next one by friends of the family. It often took her a year or more to finish one, however, and they tended to stay in the family, in the rooms of the children of this aunt or that. Sometimes Dahlia just placed them in a large biscuit box she had at home, and only took them out if you asked her.

Sunchita had once asked her if she could make a picture of something in particular, a picture of children she knew, queuing up and travelling on an aeroplane. Sunchita had asked for this very fervently, but Dahlia-aunty had laughed and said she would make that for her, one of these days. That day had not yet come. I had one of Dahlia's tapestries on my wall at home, and I had named every single figure in the image, and had a good idea of their relation to each other, the stories they were embarked upon.

Dahlia was busy in a corner of the salon, her head bent over her half-finished work. She heard me coming in, and called to me. There was no one else in the room, and I went to sit by her. She tutted, and smoothed my hair; she took a sweet-smelling folded handkerchief from the short sleeve of the dark blue blouse under her sari. She spat a little into it, and wiped my cheeks, one after the other. I must have been smudged from the street. 'Little urchin,' she said.

'Dahlia-aunty,' I said, and told her all about the *Roots* game we had been playing. I went into details. She listened patiently, laughing sometimes.

'I wondered what you were all doing,' she said. 'Nani came down from upstairs where she had been dressing the mango to dry, and said that she had never been so shocked. She saw a group of street-urchins tearing up and down the street, making a terrible din, and she thought that never had such a thing been heard of in Dhanmondi.'

'And it was us, wasn't it, Dahlia-aunty?' I said happily. I took her hand, and pulled the thimble off her forefinger; that silver top joint of the finger was fascinating to me, and I could only think of it as a sort of toy. I loved to put my finger into it, and twirl it about.

'She called down to me, and I went up, and then the whole gang of you rushed past, and I said to Nani, "I think I know one or two of those street-urchins."'

'Are we in trouble?' I asked.

Dahlia held up her needle to the light, licked the end of the blue thread, rethreaded the needle. She unsmilingly held out her hand, and I, smilingly, took the thimble off my too-thin finger. Instead of putting it on the palm of the hand she held out, I reached around and put it on the finger of her left hand; an intimate, professional thing to do, like a servant's task. She gave way: she smiled, and gave me a kiss.

29

'Who are those boys that you play with?' she said.

'I told you once,' I said, exasperated. I ran through the names, but she stopped me.

'Assad,' she said. 'Is that the little boy who lives three houses away?'

'I don't like him,' I said. 'I don't like him at all. He wanted to be the slave-owner, but everyone said I should do it, and he cried at first, but now he just wants to be another slave-owner. He doesn't play the game properly.'

'But he lives, doesn't he, three houses away? I mean, to the left, up the road, towards the main road?'

I thought, and then agreed.

'Saadi,' she said, 'I want you to promise me that you won't go to that boy's house, and you won't ask him here. You can play with him in the street, if there are lots of other children, like today, but don't go to his house, and don't have anything to do with his big brothers, or his father, or any of his family. Can you promise me that?'

I promised. 'I don't like him,' I said. 'I don't want to go to his old house, anyway.'

'Has he asked you?'

'No,' I had to admit.

'If he asks you, don't go,' Dahlia-aunty said. 'Your grandfather wouldn't like it. You know why. Now. I've been hard at work all afternoon – my fingers are red raw, look. Shall we have our tea, just you and I?'

I felt I had made a solemn and binding contract with my aunt, something which was beyond my sisters' capacity, and it was with an adult's serious walk that I went to the kitchen to call for tea and biscuits. If a guest had brought some or the kitchen had made some, there might be semai, chumchum, or rosogallai. These were the sweets that my aunt and I liked to eat together.

When my aunt said to me that I was not to play with Assad, and that I knew the reason why, she spoke the truth. At that time, there was only one reason why we did not associate with people of the neighbourhood, and that reason was known to everyone in the house, from the oldest visitors from the village down to the smallest child. It came to us as we woke, and was with us when we went to bed. We understood very well the reason why a child was forbidden our company. When Dahlia gave me this instruction I understood very well that it must have been his father who had sided with the Pakistanis.

4.

In Dhanmondi, where my grandfather lived, associations between neighbours were generally relaxed and easy. A gardener or a chauffeur would be lent without a thought; the women went between houses all day long. This was even true of the president of the country, Sheikh Mujib, whose house was four away from Khandekar-nana's house. My mother used to tell the story of going to visit Mujib's daughter, Sheikh Hasina, at her father's house, to find her in a terrible rage. She had been expecting a certain number of bags of chilli to be sent up from their estate in the country; the bags had arrived, but there were two short. 'There should be two more! Two more!' Sheikh Hasina had shouted, over and over. She barely paused in her rage to greet my mother.

'Imagine that,' my mother said. 'Her father is the president of the country, and she was angry for the lack of two bags of chilli, which she could well afford to buy from the market.'

But there were some families in the neighbourhood who walked out alone, with their heads held high; we did not know them, and we did not lend our servants to them; we did not greet them, and my grandfather said their names were unfamiliar to him. There were a number of families like this. If the children of such a family walked out with their ayah, they would walk in a regimented way, in their best clothes, looking neither to left nor to right. That expression, with a head held high, not scanning the

31

horizon but directed forward, like a horse with blinkers, was characteristic of all of them. When the gate of their house was opened, and a car drove out, with some older members of the family in it, you saw it then, that upright, distant, ignoring expression. They would not catch the eyes of anyone in the street. You could recognize these families. They dressed beautifully, dustlessly, in conventional and traditional ways. My aunts mostly put their clothes together from this and that; Mary-aunty thought nothing of borrowing her brother Pultoo-uncle's stained painting jacket to wear on top, if she was cold.

'Why can't you dress like Nadira?' Nani would say to her daughters, if they seemed to be going too far – if, say, she recognized an old pinstriped jacket of Nana's on Era's back on a cold January morning.

'Like Nadira?' Era would say, astonished.

Unlike Nadira, whose passion for clothes and makeup was legendary, they all shuffled about in old pairs of chappals, or slippers trodden down at the heel. It was accepted that they did. But Nani would not ask why her daughters could not dress like those neighbours of theirs. Those other families were immaculate in appearance, and they dressed as if they were living in the year 1850. They were the only ones in the neighbourhood where the women wore veils before their faces, where the men wore a covering on their heads. Without his tupi, I had not recognized the boy Assad for the type that he was.

These families mixed with each other, but not with us. To see the men with their friends was always unexpected; then they were at ease, greeting, laughing, chatting quite easily, their wives and sisters to one side. For those moments, despite their immaculate clothes, they resembled our own families, but of course they were not like them at all. And then they would say goodbye, and without warning, the men would resume that remote gaze of theirs. They would not acknowledge their nearest neighbours, and their nearest neighbours would ignore them, too. It was as if there were two cities laid on top of one another, each quite invisible to the other, each engaging only with its own sort.

A child knew what these people had done. They had taken money from the Pakistanis; they had betrayed their own kind; they had worked on behalf of the foreigners. They had taken the wrong side in the war, and that would never be forgotten. They had fled, often, to Pakistan, and had returned with the amnesty, buying a big house in Dhanmondi with the money they had made out of threatening Hindus and denouncing intellectuals. That was what we all believed of them. 'If everyone had their just deserts,' my aunts would say, 'such a person would not be living opposite your grandfather. They would be in jail.' And yet explaining to Assad that he must leave us and must play with his own kind was beyond me. He came from a family we could not mix with, and I did not like him. But I could not banish him on my own.

5.

During the week we lived at home and I went to school. We had no car and no television, and there were only the six of us: my mother, my father, my two sisters, my brother and myself. It was quiet in our house, and my mother's attention was all on my father's needs. My brother Zahid was to become an engineer, and his serious spirit filled the house in the evenings. I was to become a lawyer, like my father and grandfather, but although my head was bent over my books, I was only pretending to get on with my work. At school, my teachers were always shouting at me and throwing pieces of chalk at my head when they saw that I was daydreaming. My sister Sunchita was eleven months older than I, and was in the same class. She was always being held up as an example to me, with her eagerness to read, her love of studying; in the bosoms of my teachers, the memory of my serious, intelligent, practical brother Zahid was just as warm, although he was ten years older than I was. My teachers could show me that

33

I was not as good a student as Sunchita, who basked in the praise, and they were certain that I would not grow up to match Zahid. I knuckled down – and pretended to concentrate on the picture book of geography. The boy I sat at a desk with tugged our shared copy back into his half, and I kicked him.

At school and at home, pretending to work, I was thinking only of one thing. I was thinking of my chicken, Piklu. Piklu had a carefree life compared to mine. He woke up and made a brave little leap from the brink of Choto-mama's chicken coop into the garden. There would be fresh seeds to peck at, fresh worms to eat. He would puff out his little feathers, and go to explore the new morning. And that was all he had to do all day long. I worried that he would miss me. He would look about to see if I was there, but there would be only Atish, to whom one chicken was much the same as another.

My weeks were filled with worry on Piklu's behalf. While I was not there, he might eat a poisonous berry by mistake, not knowing the difference. Or a cat might get into the garden and kill him. This had happened once before, and the neighbour whose cat it was had merely apologized and told my grandfather that these things would happen. The cat must have returned to its owner with a prowling, sated gait, blood around its mouth and its whiskers adorned with fluffy yellow feathers. They must have known what it had done, but they had not cared. I could not endure that such a thing might happen to Piklu.

There were other dangers that might fall on him while I was not there. But the first among these was that Piklu might forget me between Sunday night, when we left, and Friday, when we returned to my grandfather's house.

It is astonishing how fast a chicken grows. From one week to another, an almost globular chick turns into a grey bony thing, with a great beak and awkward corners, and then, no more than a week or two later, into something that resembles a chicken, its feathers puffing out. Piklu had changed every time we arrived at my grandfather's house, and I hardly recognized him. But he recognized me. When I came towards the chicken coop, Piklu separated himself from the rest of the flock and came to greet me. I recognized him from the two irregular lines down his back, and I bent down to give him some crumbs I had kept for him. He was my chicken and I was his boy. The bond between us made Shibli jealous, but it amused almost everyone else: I had said I wanted a chicken of my own, and I had bound a chicken to me by willpower.

The best *Roots* game remained the one of capture and imprisonment. That was because of what came at the end of it: the game of auctioning off the captured slaves. There was a dramatic poignancy to that, which Shibli, who played the auctioneer, never failed to exploit. First the Africans played house, quietly at home in Africa before the slave-drivers came. Then I arrived with my henchmen, cracking whips and making the Africans scream and run. Once you had touched an African on both shoulders simultaneously, they came on to your side and chased the remaining Africans until they were all transformed. Then Shibli played the auctioneer, and sold the slaves.

'What am I bid for this fine slave?' he called, as I growled and pranced. Half of the Africans had to take the role of the bidders at the auction, or it would not have worked out. 'Am I bid one thousand dollars? Two thousand? Three?' Or sometimes he would vary it by suggesting that nobody would bid more than one cent for this miserable slave, and give them away for nothing. Nobody knew what Shibli would do; the auction part of the game filled us with a terrible, inexpressible excitement. It was what we looked forward to most.

The game started almost immediately after lunch for most of us, and continued all afternoon. It began as soon as enough people were there to join in. Assad came later. His family were religious – his mother, big sisters and aunts covered their faces with a veil, and his father, uncles and brothers, like Assad, wore a cap, a tupi, on their heads. When the call to prayer was heard, five times a day, none of my family took the slightest notice, and most of my grandfather's neighbours were the same. But you could see the family of Assad hurrying home, and we knew that they all prayed constantly. For this reason Assad was never there at the start of the game. He appeared at five o'clock, between prayers; sometimes he would say that he had given his father the slip, that he had gone to the mosque but had left him behind. He seemed to have no sense of decorum; he did not know that it should have been embarrassing and shameful to him to admit to having parents at all.

Everyone in the game had seen my chicken Piklu. He was famous in the neighbourhood. Everyone – friends of my aunts, visiting cousins from the village, the children of the *Roots* game and their families – had come to see Piklu. The way he separated himself from the flock and came to greet me, but only me, was celebrated in Dhanmondi. 'Have you seen Saadi's chicken?' people would be saying, or so I imagined, all over Dhanmondi. 'You should visit. It is worth the visit.'

If the subject came up while Assad was there, he would squat on his haunches against a wall and say nothing; he would smile in a secretive, silly way, and wait for the conversation to turn to something else. He had nothing to say about my chicken. Because, of course, he could not come to see it; I was forbidden to ask him to my grandfather's garden, and I was not sure I was really allowed to include him in the game. His uncle and father had taken money from the Pakistanis, and had told them where they could find intellectuals – musicians, poets, scholars, professors, schoolteachers – to kill. Everyone knew that, and knew that they would never be prosecuted for it. So Assad, in his tupi, with his fact-hiding, knowing smile, would never be allowed to come into my grandfather's garden to see Piklu.

6.

It was easy to escape from my grandfather's house, and when Mary-aunty had put us to bed in the afternoon, I let her walk away, then started to plot my manoeuvres. The most exciting was to get out of the bedroom, cross the landing into my grandfather's room and go out on to his balcony. There might be drying pickles out there, or just my grandfather's chair. He did not rest in his room in the afternoon, but said he would work in his library, often going to sleep there in his armchair. Only once did I come into his room to find him, his legs stretched out, on the balcony. 'Churchill!' he said. But normally it was possible to leave the aunt's room, go into my grandfather's room and through on to his balcony without discovery.

I noticed, from the balcony, that the front gate had been left open when the car had been brought in. A thought came to me. In a moment I had gripped the branch of the tamarind tree, and in another I had shinned down it. The house and the garden were absolutely quiet. I sauntered out of the front gate gleefully.

A small figure in the street, a hundred or two hundred yards away, was disturbing the peace of the afternoon. A ball of red dust with arms and legs emerging, like a fight in a comic, stopped under a tree. The dust subsided, and it turned out to be Assad in white shirt and tupi, kicking up the dirt, his arms windmilling with aimless fury. I went towards him.

'I was supposed to go to the mosque,' he said. 'But I ran away and hid, and they went without me.'

'I was put to bed,' I explained. 'But I got out.'

'Where's everybody?' he said, sinking down and jogging up and down on his haunches. 'I thought everybody would be here.'

I shrugged. I thought it was possible that the others had seen Assad on his own, and decided not to come out. You could not play the *Roots* game of slave and slave-owner with only two: what role would I play, and what role would be Assad's? Other people in the game might have thought this, and remained inside their houses. My aunt had told me I was allowed to see Assad if there were plenty of other people around, but I knew she would not like it if he became a friend of mine.

Other families must have said the same thing. I was always

susceptible to pathos when I was a child. When Mary-aunty's cat gave birth to kittens, one of the kittens fell from the balcony in the night and was found dead in the morning. My sisters and I were inconsolable; we gave it a funeral and a little gravestone, and decorated the mound of the grave with flower petals. There was something noble to me about the state of being moved, and we tried to encourage Mary-aunty's cat to stand with us as we wept over the unnamed kitten; she would not, however. So, when I saw Assad in the street, kicking at the dust and trying to see if he could rotate his arms in opposite directions, I thought of everyone who had seen him alone and decided not to come out. It was a terrible but a sad business, being the son of an informer.

'Have you seen my chicken Piklu?' I said.

Assad brightened. 'No,' he said. I knew he had not.

'Do you want to see him now?' I said. Naughtiness came over me. But I felt it was in an admirable cause. I was following a higher duty than family commandments. I went behind my aunts' backs and offered friendship to Assad because he was separated from his family, and still nobody would greet him. In that moment, I assigned fine feelings to him, and a future in which we sloped off school and went fishing together.

'You're not allowed to invite me,' he said, his face falling.

'There's no one about,' I said. 'I don't care whether you come into the garden or not.'

'My father says I'm not supposed to play with you,' he said.

'Where's your father now?' I said, shocked; I had not thought that the prohibition went in both directions.

'I don't want to see your chicken, anyway,' Assad said.

'Yes, you do,' I said. 'I know you do.' I turned back to my grandfather's house, and Assad trotted beside me. 'He knows who I am,' I said. 'He comes to me whenever I go into the garden and I call his name. He'll take food from my palm. He's getting big now – he's almost a full-grown chicken.'

'Does he think you're his mother?' Assad said.

'No, he knows who I am,' I said.

'How big is he?' Assad said, as we went through the front gate of the house. 'Is he big enough to cook and eat yet?'

'No one's going to cook and eat him,' I said. 'He's not that sort of chicken. He's my chicken, my special chicken.'

'Just because he's got a name doesn't mean they won't come and get him for the pot,' Assad said. 'If they know his name and they recognize him, they might come and get him first.'

We came round the house into the garden. There was nobody there, not even Atish the gardener.

'No one would do that,' I said. Assad had let me down with his scepticism, and I was full of scorn for him now. He understood nothing; he did not understand Piklu's place in our household. He did not deserve to be introduced to Piklu. The chickens were scattered about, feeding from the ground, like walking clouds against a dark sky. They raised their heads and, just as I had promised, Piklu with the two scribbled brown lines down his back came straight to me with joy in his strut.

I had nothing to give Piklu. I felt in my pockets, but there was nothing there. He pecked enquiringly around me, walking backwards and forwards like a sentry before me. 'This is Piklu,' I said. 'Did you see how he came straight to me? That's because he recognizes me. He knows he's my chicken.'

'How do I know that's the chicken you said is yours?' Assad said. 'All I saw is a chicken that came over looking for food. It could be any chicken.'

Assad was horrible, I saw that now. But I knew that we were not horrible to horrible people. That was not the way we were. We understood that it was our responsibility to behave in civilized ways, even when we were confronted with uncivilized people. So I said, quite mildly, 'You can tell it's Piklu because he has those two lines down his back. He had those when he was a chick, straight from the egg.'

'You could just have said that,' Assad said. 'What else does your chicken do? It doesn't do anything interesting.'

'He doesn't have to do interesting things,' I said. 'He's not in

39

a circus. He's my chicken. Anyway, you don't do interesting things. I've never seen you do anything interesting. Piklu's much nicer and more interesting than you are.'

'I can do lots of interesting things. I know how to do all sorts of things you don't,' Assad said. His voice had coarsened and deepened. 'I know how . . .' He lowered himself by stages, gently, gently, towards the ground, and then, quite suddenly, his hand shot out and caught Piklu round the neck. 'I know how to kill a chicken.'

Piklu was trapped by the neck under Assad's hand; his feet were running frantically in the dust.

'The principle is the same,' Assad said. 'It's the same for anything that you want to kill. You slice through the neck –' for one moment I thought he had a knife in his pocket, that he was going to kill Piklu in front of me, but he was just slicing against Piklu's white throat with the edge of his hand '– and then it bleeds to death, quite quickly. It makes a terrible mess, my father said. Not with a small animal like a chicken. But with bigger animals, it makes a big mess.'

I knew this was true. I had seen the slaughter of a cow in the street at the festival of Eid, and walked afterwards through the slip of blood on stone, the gallons of blood churning the streets into mud, the stench filling the street, like the crowd, pressing up against you. And afterwards, the stink that came from the tanneries, down by the river. It was unavoidable if you had to take a boat from Sadarghat, and the smell of the black water was the smell of large animals being slaughtered. If you lived in Dacca, you knew the big mess that a bigger animal made when it was killed.

All at once I could move. I rushed at Assad, screaming, my fists held high, and he let Piklu go. My chicken jumped to its feet, shuffling its feathers, and ran away to the far corner of the garden. I hit Assad with both my fists in the certainty that Piklu would now never again come to me of his free will: he would remember the day that I had asked him to come to me and I had delivered him to Assad. He would remember being held down by his throat against the dirt, and the thought that he was about to die, and he would run from me. I pummelled Assad, and he hit me back, his tupi flying from his head.

Then Nani, my grandmother, was in the garden. 'Stop that at once,' she said. 'Brawling like street-urchins. Stop it. I'm ashamed of you, Saadi. What would Nana have to say? Do you think he would call you Churchill now?'

We stopped, our faces lowered towards the mud our fight had made. Grown-ups, when they interrupted our fights, had a way of insisting that we shook hands, apologized and made up with each other. It was their way. But Nani inspected Assad, his dirty shirt, his muddy hair, and the tupi lying on the leaves of a shrub, like washing laid out to dry, and made no such demand. 'I know who you are,' she said to Assad, taking his dirty head in her hands, turning it this way and that, like a shopkeeper with a fine vase. 'I want you to leave my garden now, and never come back. You should never have come into my garden. Go away.'

41

Assad went. Nani watched him go every step of the way; she followed him to the gate, and shut it behind him with her own hands. 'I don't know how that was left open,' she said. 'Saadi, go and have a bath. I'm ashamed of you.'

7.

It was our ayah's job to go and hail a cycle-rickshaw to take us, each Friday morning, from my parents' house to my grandparents'. When she opened the gates, you could see the woman who always squatted there, under the tree, breaking bricks and stones into rubble all day long; her skin was dry and white with the dust, and we were forbidden to speak to her. While our ayah was finding the cycle-rickshaw, my mother lined us up and inspected us. My sisters were wearing their best frocks; I was in my newest and whitest shirt. My brother was coming with us, unusually. He was wearing his best shirt. We knew what this meant, and before we set off, my mother asked us to behave especially well. There were people coming to Nana's from the village. They were especially looking forward to seeing us, and we should not disappoint them by rolling in the mud, by saying that we were bored and could we watch the television, or by stuffing rice into our cheeks at the dinner table and pretending we were rats. That was always disgusting for other people, but it would be very disappointing for Nana's visitors to see us behaving in such a way. 'That was only Saadi,' my sister Sushmita said.

My sister Sunchita whispered into my ear, 'It's the witch who's coming,' when we were safely jammed into the cycle-rickshaw – our ayah had found a good one, polished silver with a big picture of a tiger on the back. 'It's her time of year to come.' The rickshaw driver fastened his blue cotton lungi between his hairy, bony knees, above the cycle crossbar, spat into the dry earth of the street, and we set off.

Our great-grandmother was called by Sunchita and me 'the witch' for no very good reason, except that she scared us. She was the last of the two widows of Nana's father. I could just about remember the other one, and what they had been like. They had lived together where they had always lived, in Nana's father's house in the village. Nana's father was the last person in the family who had married more than one woman; the question had never arisen afterwards, and now never would. The elder of the two had died when I was very small and, until then, they had come to see Nana once a year, around this time. The surviving one had carried on. Nana never travelled from Dacca to her village, although he sent small presents whenever any of his children went there in the summer. Nana always chose saris for her; he liked her to wear white saris with a thin band of colour, of blue or purple, at the edge, or sometimes a band of silver. (I could still remember her and the elderly senior wife, matching in their white and purple saris.) And the second one, the survivor, came to Dacca every year, in the summer, where she frightened, without knowing it, her great-grandchildren.

At Nana's house, everything was in a state of confusion. The gardener's boy was cleaning the car with a bucket of water; Atish was weeding the flowerbed. In the upper windows, great white birds appeared to be plunging in the half-light; beds were being changed and aired. My great-grandmother had arrived, and had found fault. The servants, who were used to their own ways, did not look forward to her visits any more than I did. Attention fell on her in unwelcome ways; attention was simultaneously taken from me, and neither of us enjoyed it.

We were led upstairs in our best clothes, and there in her room was my great-grandmother. The maid who always served her was already hard at work, brushing her hair; it was absolutely white – 'As white as snow,' I dreamily said to myself, a comparison from English books and not from experience. She could keep her maid hard at it all day long, going from one intimate task to another. While her hair was being brushed, she was at work preparing paan.

She had her own pestle and mortar for this, and would prepare paan to chew; sometimes Nani took some, out of politeness, to give her mother-in-law some company. She pounded away at the tiny red rubble in her wooden bowl, the wooden pestle long since stained as if with blood. Her task was like that of the woman stone-breaker outside her house, but fragrant, elegant, clean and beautiful. She did not trust or like preparations of paan that had been made by anyone else. She carried the ingredients round in small pouches, making it out of dried leaves, pebble-like substances, samples of mysterious red matter, all just as she liked it. Her pestle and mortar, as well as the wooden clogs she always wore that gave you warning of her approach, were somehow carried over from the senior wife. She seemed to be carrying out a dead woman's wishes, and she scared the life out of me.

We submitted to being kissed by a paan-smelling old mouth, and my mother reminded her who we were, and how old we were now. She seemed to take it all in, nodding over her stained moustaches. But then she immediately started explaining who had done what to whom in the village. She lived in a large property, given to both women by my grandfather, and she was the centre of village complaint and litigation. Everyone had always come to the pair of them with disputes, and nowadays she passed down the law without hesitation.

(Nana had a story about his mothers' intrusions. He told it endlessly. It seemed that a village couple had decided to give their new baby daughter a Western name, and had somehow heard of 'Irene'. Unexpectedly, the mother gave birth not to one daughter, but to a pair of twins, and the couple could not think of a suitable second name for some time. Then they were struck by inspiration, and decided to call the second daughter 'Urine'. This was one of the many occasions on which my great-grandmothers descended into the private lives of the villagers, and told them what they could not do, brooking no contradiction. Nana could never remember what the daughters were called in the end, with the agreement of his father's two wives.)

The stories of litigation and irritation reached their first pause, and the enquiries had run their course into how Zahid was growing up into a fine young man, and I would be a lawyer like my father and grandfather. My mother had gently reminded her that Sushmita and Sunchita would have their own professions, too. We were permitted to go downstairs, but only to sit quietly and to read a book, not to turn on the television, not to trouble the servants, and certainly not to go out and run in the garden, just underneath the window of Great-grandmother's room.

I wanted to see Piklu, my chicken, but I knew better than to disobey my mother when the witch was there. We filed downstairs and took up our books in the salon, sitting on two cream-and-brown sofas at right angles to each other, Sunchita reading a long sentimental novel, Sushmita a Feluda detective story, and my brother Zahid a physics textbook, which seemed to give him as much pleasure as anything. From time to time, Sunchita would sigh affectedly at some occurrence in her book, and even remark on an event that had moved her. I had my book, too, but I could not stay still. I thought of Piklu, out there; I did not know if he would come to greet me, or whether I would remain unforgiven for what Assad had done to him the previous weekend. Piklu changed from week to week, although now he was a proper, grown-up chicken, as big as his mother, and I did not want to be separated from him. From time to time I leapt up from the scratchy wool sofa, going to the window to see if I could see Piklu. But I could not. The other chickens were pottering about, pecking at the dirt as usual, but Piklu must have been inside the chicken coop, waiting for me to come.

8.

'Ah, children,' Mary-aunty said, coming into the salon. She, too, was wearing her best clothes, with a gold band down the edge of her sari. 'I hope you're all being good. Oh dear.' She fluttered, and left. In a moment Dahlia came in. She came straight to me, picked up the book I was reading from my lap and looked at the title. Ignoring the others, she gave me a kiss on my nose; she shook her head, and hurried out again.

The aunts came in, singly and in pairs, and found some reason to address me before leaving in an absent way. I could not account for it. My aunts had different favourites, and sometimes our own gestures of fondness were not returned; Sushmita had thought Nadira, with her dramatic entrances and her immaculate appearance, was marvellous, but Nadira, before she got married and went to Sheffield, was at best indifferent to the small, impressed offerings of gaze and giggle that Sushmita laid at her feet. Today every aunt came in and, one after another, stroked my head or called me a little sweetie. It was as if they wanted something from me. It was unusual in any circumstance: when Great-grandmother was there, making demands and criticizing the household, calling for people to brush her hair and listen to her stories, we children were used to being ushered into a quiet corner and expected to remain silent. The attention I was getting was pleasing, but unnerving. I wondered whether I was about to get a present.

'And he is studying at college now,' Great-grandmother said at table. She was talking about the son of a neighbour of theirs, a neighbour in the country. 'Studying to be an engineer. He has made a good success of his life. When you consider who his father is. There was constant trouble with his father. Running wild. And now he is going to Libya,' she finished, hunching over her plate.

'Fateh is going to Libya?' Nana said, puzzled. He remembered the farmer, his youth, running wild.

'Libya?' Era said.

'Not Fateh,' Great-grandmother said, her brilliant white hair combed back now. 'Fateh could never go to Libya. Fateh stays where he was born. His son, he is going to Libya. He is studying at college. Studying to be an engineer. And afterwards, he is going to Libya.'

There was a satisfied pause. The dining-room door swung open, and in came a succession of dishes, steaming hot. All at once, the table broke into conversation.

'Were you at your college today?' Dahlia called across to Pultoo-uncle.

'No, because—'

'And Mahmood had a great success today,' my mother called across to Nani, gesturing at my father who, in honour of a great-grandparent, had come, for once, to dinner on Friday.

'I'm so pleased for him,' Nani said. 'Era, did you hear what your sister was saying?'

'Yes, Mama,' Era said. 'A success, today . . . I was just about to say . . .'

It was mystifying. The lids of the dishes were taken off, in a shining line down the long table; the richest of the dishes before Nana. 'Good, good,' he said, poking in it with the serving spoon in his usual way; it was as if he suspected the most delicious parts to be always hidden deep in the dish. 'Good. Chicken.'

Around the table, there was a nervous little spasm of conversation, and I had the sense of aunt turning to aunt, and smiling shamefully at me. 'Do have some, Saadi,' Mary-aunty said. 'It's especially for your great-grandmother, since she has come all this way to see us.'

A horrible thought came to me. 'Where did the chicken come from?' I said to Nana. 'Nana, what is this chicken?'

But I had been shunted down a place by the arrival of my great-grandmother, and he affected not to hear my shrill demand. 'Nana,' I said. 'Nana.'

'Quiet, Saadi,' Bubbly-aunty said, next to me. 'Don't scream in people's ears. It's a chicken from the garden, as usual.'

'Which one?' I said. 'Which chicken are we eating?'

'I really don't know,' Bubbly said. 'I really don't know the difference between one chicken and another. They'd be very happy, I'm sure, if they knew they were going to make such a lovely dinner for all of us. Now, I'm sure you're not going to be a bad little boy. I'm sure you're going to be a good little boy, and eat your dinner, aren't you?'

In my family, we did not leap up and push our chairs over; we did not scream and denounce our relations; we did not punch and pummel the servants, even the ones who had seized our pet chickens and put them in the pot without a second thought. We did not run howling out into the garden in search of our lost chickens. What we did was push the dish away when it came to us, and say, with murder in our voices, 'No, thank you. I don't care to eat a friend of mine.'

'What did he say?' Great-grandmother said.

'I didn't hear,' Nana said. 'Pay no attention, and everything will be quite all right.'

9.

I sat in mutinous silence all through dinner. I would not look at or answer my great-grandmother, for whose sake Piklu had been killed and eaten. I promised myself I would never speak to her again, not until she died like the other one, which would be soon. And when dinner was over, I gabbled out the formula asking for permission to get down from the table, and went swiftly out of the front door into the street. It was still light, and my shadow went before me as I walked, shivering and dancing like a puppet, making its own dance, as I tried to walk like a big man down the Dhanmondi street, trying my best to walk like a slave-owner, to walk as a talking car would walk, to walk down my grandfather's street like Hungry Bear.

3: Altaf and Amit

1.

The best place to watch what was happening in the street was from my grandfather's first-floor balcony. The houses in the street were fronted by high walls, dusted with green lichen, for security. But the balcony on the first floor was high enough to see over. From there, you could see visitors approaching. It might be a family member returning: Nana in his red Vauxhall, driven by Rustum, or my father in a cycle-rickshaw, laden with papers, or some aunts returning from a visit in the neighbourhood. As you negotiated your way between heavy jars of pickles, or slices of mango laid out on kula to dry, you could see if there was a war going on in the street between children of the neighbourhood. Sometimes, when I was very young I would see Sheikh Mujib sweep by in his big official car, with a policeman on a motorbike driving just before. And you knew that he was the prime minister of the country. I never forgot that sight.

Or there might be visitors. Mr Khandekar-nana came sometimes, simply, on foot, with his wife and a son or two. Pultoo-uncle's friends Kajol and Kanaq would arrive with their folders of art under their arms, sticking out from either side of a cycle-rickshaw. You could hear them arguing from a hundred yards away: they always turned up in a towering passion, appealing to anyone in the house to settle the dispute by taking one side or the other. From Nana's balcony, through the branches of the

49

eat as much as we could. My sister Sushmita would stay inside, not getting up the whole day, complaining about her headache and her exhaustion, lying in the dark as awed country aunts brought her tea and soft, white, affectionate things on small plates to tempt her appetite.

And Sunchita would pick her moment. She would run out into the mango orchard, a book and a stolen red silk pillow from the dusty salon under her arm. She would find a tree with low-lying branches, and jump on to the lowest, gripping the trunk of the tree. She would climb up into the dark foliage where the red mangoes hung like Chinese lanterns. She would find a place to rest her back, and then reach forward from time to time in the dappled interior light, plucking a ripe mango from its long stalk. She would pummel the fruit, and pinch a hole at the bottom, and suck the flesh out whole. All the time, in this light-and-dark-strewn hiding place, her concentration would be on the book she held. Wedged into a tree in a mango orchard, the red silk cushion behind her back, she could read for hours, the distant shouts of farmers and cousins not disturbing her, hardly noticing the song of the birds sitting at rest, like her, in the trees.

5: A Party at Sufiya's

1.

First, some history.

In 1947, the British left India, and it was split in two: India and Pakistan.

Pakistan was to be for the Muslims, and India for the rest. Many people died making their way to their new homeland, killed by gangs on the railways or on the roads.

Pakistan was a single nation, but anyone could see that it was split in two. To the left was West Pakistan, where they ruled, and spoke Urdu, and wrote in an alphabet that flowed like water under wind.

To the right was East Pakistan, where the Bengalis lived. They spoke Bengali, which chatters like a falling xylophone, and is written in an alphabet that looks like a madman trying to remember a table's shape.

The two new countries – India and Pakistan, East and West – they looked on the map like a broad-shouldered ape with two coconuts, one on its right shoulder, one under its left armpit.

The new government wanted to make Bengal speak and write in its language, Urdu. They also wanted to change Bengali so that it would, in future, be written in the flowing script of Urdu.

There were riots in Bengal, and in 1952 some students from the Bengal Language Movement were killed in Dacca. My parents were among those protesting, and were placed in jail overnight, to their subsequent great happiness.

In the years afterwards, the Bengali language, Bengali poetry, music and culture became important for those who wanted independence for the Bengali nation. It also became a point of honour for the government in Pakistan to observe and suppress the Bengali language wherever possible. Governments went on trying to persuade Bengalis to write their language in the Urdu script.

The situation could not continue, for one reason. There were very many more speakers of Bengali in the whole nation of Pakistan than there were speakers of Urdu. And yet Bengali culture was suppressed and its language occupied an insecure position. In the 1960s Mujibur Rahman, who was the head of a political party, the Awami League, looked forward to a day when the Bengali majority might vote for a Bengali leader of Pakistan as a whole. There seemed no reason why this should not happen. It would be interesting to see what would happen in the Pakistani capital when this came about.

In the meantime, in the respectable houses of Dhanmondi and elsewhere in Dacca, it was considered patriotic and, indeed, very enjoyable to hold parties in which Bengali music was played and Bengali poetry recited. The daughters of the houses walked openly past policemen in their Pakistani uniforms, holding sheaves of music, chattering boldly like singing birds. Sometimes Sheikh Mujib came, too, when he was not being sent to prison.

2.

This afternoon, for instance, there is to be a party at Sufiya's house. Sufiya is a good-hearted woman, and very popular in Dacca. She is friends with everyone, from Syed Hosain, the advocate, and Khandekar, the lawyer, to Sheikh Mujib himself, poets and painters and folklore specialists; she has a word to say to the musicians, always knows a kind word to settle the children and stop them running around too violently. Her daughters, Sultana and Saeeda, do much of the hard work of hospitality, welcoming people, arranging the food, making sure everyone is seated with someone they will have something to say to. At every party of Sufiya's, everyone must meet somebody new to them, as well as greet their old friends. The hard work is her daughters', because Sufiya's role at the party is to read her poetry. She is a famous poet, and people labour to secure invitations to her open house. They do not have to labour hard. Sufiya likes to meet new people, of every sort.

It is four o'clock. The weather is oppressive and steamy, the air thick and still. In the salon, Sultana and Saeeda sit, fanning themselves with broad leaves from the garden. The plain terracotta pots about the sitting room are filled with simple white flowers. Sultana, at eighteen, has just started her English degree; her younger sister is a gifted artist. They will welcome the artists and the musicians, the politicians, too, between them. Sufiya does not like to be found waiting for the first of her guests: she thinks it makes a better party if she descends when a few guests have already gathered. At the moment she is in the kitchen, checking the Bengali cakes the cooks have made: pati shaptha, pancake roll stuffed with coconut halwa, the fudge-like borfi, puli pitha, the dumplings. She likes to be sure of everything in advance, and is going over everything at the last moment. If she leaves it any longer, Sultana remarks to her sister, she is going to be caught out by the first guests, and will be deprived of her entrance. But there are still the bought sweets to go over and count, the things the confectioner supplies: chumchum dusted with icing sugar, black gulab-jamun with a secret interior of brilliant pink, the rolled yellow balls of laddu, sandesh like toy bricks, some with a coat of silver. 'Is there enough chanachur?' Sufiya's voice can be heard from the kitchen. She has, surely, asked after this before, and is now going over old ground. Now there is the sound of a cycle-rickshaw outside the gates: the first guest is here, and Sufiya must hurry herself upstairs to hide for the first half-hour. She hurries through the house in her simple white cotton sari. The house has french windows to the front. The terrace at the front has two sofas, and a bookcase. More bookcases in the hall can be seen from the path through the front garden, and even, through the openwork iron gates, from the road, as the french windows are open. Sufiya's disappearance upstairs must be noticed.

In the hallway, the maid is occupied dusting the shelves as the first guests come up the stone path, between flowerbeds, under the coconut palms and lychee trees to either side. They come in through the half-open door. It is Salim, his wife and his three children. He is a schoolmaster. His daughters are pretty little things, in white party dresses puffed out with ribbons, but very noisy. Salim's wife is a nice woman, though she is Bihari; born speaking Urdu, she prides herself – prides herself perhaps too much – on the way she has transformed herself into a Bengali. 'You are quite one of us,' Sufiya had once said generously, and something in the way Mona has dressed herself today makes Sultana say the same thing now. Still, she hopes that Mona will not try to emphasize her acquired Bengali-ness by offering to sing a Nazrul song later in the party. She has never lost her foreign accent, and the last time she did it, the audience giggled until Mona could no longer pretend not to hear, her hands clenched to the grim end of the song. 'Would the girls like to play in the garden?' Sultana asks. 'My mother will be down soon.' And there is the young doctor, a new friend of Sufiya's – she collects young doctors; he is with his new wife, only six months married. Salim and his wife Mona stand with the doctor and his wife. They do not know each other, but they talk very easily, and in a moment, one of them suggests sitting down. Salim hands his wife to a chair, and Sultana sees from his solicitude that Mona, again, is pregnant. She wonders whether to say anything.

The guests come promptly. Sultana does not immediately recognize the two young men who arrive next, both very clean and innocent-looking, but they announce themselves as the musicians, and then of course she remembers. 'Is Nadira here yet?' the tall one asks. 'She asked us to come at the same time as her, but I am not sure we know what time she was planning to arrive.' Saeeda assures them that they are very welcome, whether Nadira has arrived yet or not, and makes a special point of calling for tea for the pair of them – they seem to have walked to the party. And then there is Khandekar and his wife; they greet Sultana and Saeeda quickly, circumspectly, before going over to make a point of greeting the two musicians. Everyone knows that the musicians are tenants of Mrs Khandekar. In Dacca in 1968, that is of not much concern.

Now there are enough guests here, there is a commotion at the top of the stairs, and Sufiya, smiling in her owl-like glasses, gathering her simple white sari to her throat, is coming down. The guests gather at the entrance to the salon to greet her. 'You have seen the paintings?' she says, but nobody has: they did not know that there were to be paintings today. The art has been laid out in the courtyard of the house, on tables arranged into an L-shape. Sufiya leads the way through the back windows. There are views of Old Dacca by, she explains, a promising young artist from the university. They are done in charcoal and pencil. 'I hope that Zainul is coming,' Sufiya says; Zainul Abedin is her great friend from Calcutta days, a great painter. Everyone knows his ink drawings of the Calcutta famine; all Dacca, and all India, too. 'I do so want to hear his opinion.' These are pinned against board and, in the humid afternoon, are starting to curl up at the edges. Interspersed with the drawings, Sufiya has placed some folk art – pottery and small tapestry work. They are simple things, bearing images of farmers and milkmaids, but interesting. She gathered them on a trip last month into Jessore. The guests admire them, picking them up and turning them over. The peasant art is having more success than the skilful, elaborate drawings of corners of Old Dacca. Sufiya's poetry, too, is simple and unadorned. She likes the simple statement, and the line that anyone can understand. Her poetry is like these white pottery jugs, simple, useful, but pleasant to handle.

Now there are more guests: Sufiya goes back into the salon to

100

greet them with tea and cakes and lemon water. It would not do if she were in the back room, fussing over cakes, when Sheikh Mujib arrived, or even Zainul Abedin. She keeps an eye on the degree of disruption at the gates, signalling an important guest, as one waiting for the monsoon to break.

'Sufiya,' a new guest says, after she has been welcomed – she is the wife of an architect, recently returned from Europe, 'do you know those men?'

'Everyone is welcome,' Sufiya says. 'The gates are open, you know.'

'The men standing outside,' the architect's wife says, 'I thought they must be . . .' She gathers her shawl to her throat. She is not quite clear what she thought they were.

Sufiya goes into the hallway, and out through the front door. There are, as the architect's wife said, two men standing there. Their clothes distinguish them from Sufiya's guests. They are standing there as people dismount from their rickshaw and come in. The guests lower their heads as they pass: the men stare insolently into the faces of the guests. She keeps open house, and sometimes people she does not know arrive, and are very welcome if they are interested in Bengali culture, take an interest in the pottery, sit quietly and appreciatively during poetry and music. These are not people of that sort. They are wearing salwaar kameez, the Bihari shirt with a collar and buttons; her other guests, if they are wearing traditional dress, are wearing the Bengali shirt without collar. Some, like the architect, are wearing quite glamorously embroidered shirts, but the people outside are wearing everyday, even rather dusty clothes. They are standing on either side of the gate without looking in at the party or at each other. They do not seem to have come to a party at all.

'Karim,' Sufiya says, not raising her voice, and her darowan, the gatekeeper, is next to her, 'have you seen those men?' She does not need to say who they are. Karim has been with her for twenty years, and he knows what to do. He walks out, just as three of Hosain's daughters are piling out of a rickshaw, Nadira in the front. They know better than to linger, though the scene is interesting.

'What are you doing?' Karim is saying. 'Why are you loitering here? You have no right to be threatening Madam's guests like this. Be off with you.'

'We're not threatening anyone,' one of the men says. 'Got a perfect right to stand where we like.'

'Go and stand somewhere else,' the darowan says. 'You're not welcome here.'

'If you don't like it,' the other says – he has broken teeth, stained from paan, and now cleans his mouth, spits on the ground, 'if you don't like it, you can complain. To the relevant authorities.'

No one doubts that the relevant authorities are precisely the people who have sent these two men to stand outside Sufiya's house. Mona, Salim's Bihari wife, has turned decorously away; she has let herself be absorbed in greeting Nadira and her sisters, Dahlia and Mary. Salim has seen that the familiar debate is happening at Sufiya's gates, and has come forward to add his weight of persuasion to Sufiya's steward's. When Sufiya next looks, the men have been talked into leaving. They had carried out their task, after all.

As if waiting for the departure of the goons, the gates open, and in steps Sheikh Mujib, followed by one of his daughters. His famous simplicity is evident here: there is no car outside, and he has, as usual, walked the five hundred yards from his house to Sufiya's. He smiles to right and left, and comes through the gate as Karim, the darowan, lowers his head and says, 'Salaam.' Sufiya comes forward to greet this most important of her guests. Behind her, on the veranda, the guests have risen from their seats, and inside, the chatter is ceasing as people come to the window. 'Now the party can commence,' she says. 'I am so happy that you have come.'

'I would not dream of missing it,' he says. 'Some wretched people tried to inconvenience me, to prevent my attendance. But

I would not let them stand in the way of my old friend's party.'
He presents his daughter.

Everyone has stood up, and Sufiya takes Sheikh Mujib around the party, first to the veranda, then inside to the salon, presenting him to everyone – to her daughters, to Salim and his wife, who lowers her eyes, to Nadira and her sisters, to doctors and architects and poets and painters, even to the musicians. The Friend of Bengal is easy and approachable, and greets the musicians with particular kindness. 'Now sit, sit,' he says to Sufiya, almost forcing her into her chair; it is his usual gesture, to insist that Sufiya should sit before him and, after demurral, she does so. The other guests, however, wait for Sheikh Mujib and his daughter to sit before taking their seats again. On cue, Sufiya's servants start to circulate with plates of sweets and cake, and cups of tea. Nadira, Altaf and Amit gather, and in a moment they start on a song, its long sweet lines over the tabla like rain on a river. In five minutes, Sheikh Mujib rises again, goes outside, and admires the pottery, taking a small crowd of guests with him, each with a cup in hand.

The doctor greets Hosain, the lawyer. They live close to each other, and regularly take an afternoon walk around the lake in Dhanmondi. The doctor – capable, brief in conversation and intelligent – is in fact the man Hosain goes to for advice and help, even on family matters. He stands loose-limbed, his face defined by his small round glasses; he gleams like a health-conscious revolutionary.

'I am glad to see you,' Hosain says.

'I thought I would see you here,' the doctor says.

Then Hosain plunges straight in. 'I am concerned about Pultoo,' he says. 'My youngest boy. He shows no aptitude for anything. He does not do well at his classes. All he does is draw, all day long. His teacher says he sits and dreams during mathematics, he gazes ahead without concentrating in all his other lessons, and if he seems to be working, he is really sketching something. He draws all the time. I do not know what to do with him.'

'You say he has no aptitude for anything,' the doctor says.

'Yes, that's right,' the lawyer says.

'But he draws all the time.'

'Yes, he can't be stopped – he draws in the notebook he is supposed to be working out sums in, during mathematics.'

'Is he good at drawing?' the doctor says.

'Yes, I think so. He makes his classmates laugh by drawing them, and his teachers, and sometimes he draws the view from his classroom window. And he made a very good drawing of the gardener at home. Yes, I think he can draw.'

'I don't understand why you say he has no aptitude for anything,' the doctor says. 'It sounds as if he has an aptitude for art.'

'Oh, for art,' the lawyer says. 'That is not a very useful aptitude.'

'The world needs a good artist more than it needs an incompetent engineer,' the doctor says.

'I so agree,' says Sufiya, passing. 'Now, have you seen the art in the garden? I was so hoping that Zainul would come. He promised he would come early. I so wanted to show him some drawings of a young friend of mine, and Saeeda, my daughter, you know, she is painting so beautifully nowadays. I particularly wanted him to come early. It is really too bad.'

'But there he is,' the doctor says. He looks surprised. 'There he is, talking to my brother's daughter.'

'Oh, that is too bad,' Sufiya says again, but affectionately. 'He always does that. He always sneaks in quietly, with no word of hello, and then finds a quiet corner. He really is too bad.'

You would never know that Zainul Abedin is who he is, if you saw him at a party. He arrives quietly, with nobody knowing; he finds a quiet corner, with nobody much in it, just an old friend. He would spend any gathering perfectly happily talking to small children or to somebody's aunt, visiting from the country, talking about their concerns and small worries, listening about the failure of the crops or a pet chicken or a girl's best friend, now her worst enemy. He listens with his full attention; sometimes only much later, years sometimes, does his new friend discover that this kindly gentleman, his fingers stained with paint and nicotine, was the great painter. Sometimes never; and once or twice Sufiya has found that her oldest friend Zainul Abedin has been to a party of hers, never said hello, sat on a stool in a dark corner, chatted to hardly anyone, and departed quietly, having had, he would tell her later, a very nice time.

He is sitting with a small girl, the niece of the doctor, in a party dress. Their full attention is on something Zainul Abedin is holding on his knee.

'You see,' he is saying, 'I came on a bus today.'

She looks.

'And this was my ticket,' he says.

She looks at the small piece of paper he is holding on his knee.

'And it has print on one side, but not so much on the other side,' he says. 'So here's a pen, and here's some paper' – it is only one inch by two, the bus ticket, hardly that, even – 'and the pen wants to draw something, but it doesn't know what it wants to draw. What is it going to draw?'

The small girl looks at the pen, poised above the bus ticket resting on this gentleman's knee, and says something into her fist, very shyly.

'Is it going to draw Papa?' the painter says. The girl nods, and quickly, with six, seven strokes, a scribble and some dabs, like the nib pecking at the paper, there he is; her father, a thin, serious fellow, leaning over to catch what his brother-in-law is saying, not at all aware that he has been caught for ever in this attitude on the back of a Dacca bus-ticket; his portrait, by Zainul Abedin, given to his daughter. The girl's eyes grow wide – she reaches out with both hands. She recognizes her father in those few strokes. For a moment it had been just strokes of the pen, and then it was her father, all at once. 'Do you want it?' Zainul Abedin says. 'You're very welcome, but, just one moment.' He waves the bus ticket around in the air, three times, to dry the ink. 'And here you are.'

'My dear old friend,' Sufiya says. 'Up to your old tricks again. Now,' turning to the small girl, 'let me get a little envelope for that. You must always keep that safe, you know. Have you been to see the drawings yet? And Saeeda would never ask herself, but she is painting so very interestingly these days, she would love to hear what you have to say.'

'I was just about to get up to find her,' Zainul Abedin says. 'But she must be busy with your guests. I can come back tomorrow.'

Elsewhere in the party, Sultana has been waylaid by Mary, her friend.

'So what happened?' she says.

'What do you mean?' Sultana says.

'You arrived at the university the other day in a large black car,' Mary says. 'I know it was Sheikh Mujib's. How is it that he is turned into your chauffeur these days?'

'He was not in the car,' Sultana says. 'He had got out earlier. All right, I'll tell you. What happened was that I was late getting up, and it was almost a quarter to nine when I left the house. I had a class on Wordsworth at nine at the university, and you know what a stickler old Das is for punctuality. So I was really thinking about whether it would not be best to go back home and tell Professor Das that I had been ill when I next saw him – but then I thought about Ma, and how I could tell her that I had missed Das on poetry just because I slept late, and I saw that would not do either. So I was really on the horns of a dilemma when a car drew up alongside me, standing on the road like a hopeless case, and the window wound down, and it was Sheikh Mujib. He said, "You look a little late to me," and I confessed that I was late, and that I had a class at the university. So he said, "I can easily give you a lift," and I was so grateful, and I saw that it was really my only chance to get to university on time, that I accepted straight away. Never mind what Ma would say, I thought, when she heard that I was inconveniencing the Friend of Bengal. But it was much, much worse than I thought, because after five minutes of chatting about what I was up to, and whether I preferred Wordsworth to Keats, because Sheikh Mujib had read Keats when he was young, in Calcutta, and he was saying that, really, he thought there was no poetry in the world to touch the "Ode to the Nightingale", and I was sticking up for the "Ode to a Grecian Urn", because in my view —'

'Yes, yes,' Mary says. 'But what was the inconvenience to the Friend of Bengal – the more than usual one?'

'Well, after five minutes he said, "I am so sorry but I am going to have to leave you here – my driver will take you on to Curzon Hall, but you know, I must be punctual when I need to come here." And it was at the courthouse he was being left. I felt such a fool because, of course, Pa and Ma were talking about Sheikh Mujib being prosecuted again, and having to go to the courthouse to answer an invented case the very next day. "They may send me to jail again, or they may not send me to jail," he said to me, "but I know they will definitely send me to jail today if I don't arrive on time, and call it contempt of court. I am so sorry, my young friend, to be so discourteous as to leave you here, but the driver will take you anywhere you want to go. Don't be in a hurry, I may be here for some time." And then he got out and there was a huge crowd to meet him, and I went on. All the faces were pressed up against the glass – they wanted to see who I was, and all of that. I don't know what they thought.'

'But they didn't send him to jail,' Mary said. 'Pa was talking about it this morning, but Nadira and Dahlia were arguing about something else, and I don't think I heard properly.'

'No, he's out on bail,' Sultana said. 'I am glad to see him here. He is so nice, really. And now Ma is going to read.'

Silence falls, and Sufiya stands, a piece of paper in her hand. She begins to speak.

'"This is no time to be braiding your hair . . ."'

3.

Two days after her party, Sufiya receives some uninvited guests. They are two men. Not the two men who were seen loitering at her gates, staring insolently at her guests. But they may be assumed to have some connection with those men – perhaps their supervisors, their superiors. And these visitors have superiors, too. They come from a world where everyone has underlings and everyone has superiors, and they cannot conceive of any other existence.

Sufiya asks them in, perhaps unnecessarily. They refuse tea, and any other offering, and it is true that by the end of their conversation Sufiya would happily have slipped poison into any cup of tea she would offer them. Is it the case that she organized a gathering of individuals opposed to the government two days ago? No, it was a small meeting of friends, come together to drink tea and to listen to a little music. Nevertheless, among those attending were – one of the men, a moustachioed person with an unnerving, practised, direct gaze, extracts a clean typed sheet of names from his black leather briefcase – were well-known leaders of opposition and dissent. Who did they have in mind? The man begins to read out the names: he concludes with Sheikh Mujib's. An old friend, Sufiya says. She is aware that her daughter Sultana has come downstairs and is standing discreetly in the door of the salon, listening. She wishes she would go away: she does not want these men from the security service to recognize either of her daughters at any point in the future.

Is it the case, the other man says, clipped and neat-looking in his blue blazer and English tie, that among the topics discussed at this gathering was the founding of a dissident cultural institute? Sufiya cannot think what they are talking about, and says so. The man goes into more detail, and soon she realizes that they are referring to the room that the university is making available to any practitioners of Bengali arts. She sets her face. The men at the gate did not hear that conversation. She wonders who it was who overheard it and, for a shameful moment, her mind settles on Mona, Salim's Bihari wife. She dismisses the thought.

'Do you know it is forbidden to hold gatherings of more than twelve people without permission?' one of the men says. This may or may not be true, but is certainly one of the laws that would be applied only if the authorities wanted to stop a gathering taking place for other reasons. She does not believe that when the daughters of government ministers get married, official permission for the reception is applied for, or would ever be withheld. All the same, she acknowledges the statement, and after a few minutes, the two men run out of things to threaten her with. They stand to go. Sultana whisks herself off, out of the doorway and into the kitchen, where she cannot be seen. 'I am sorry I cannot be of more help to you,' Sufiya says sweetly, as she shows them to the door. She invited them in, after all, and they are, in some sense, guests of hers. They have the grace to look a little embarrassed at that. She shuts the door behind them, wanting to break a vase over their silly heads, and breathes deeply. Sultana comes out from the kitchen and, behind her, Hamida, the cook, both with deeply concerned expressions. No one says anything.

That was the sort of encounter which happened, with increasing frequency, in Dacca during this time, when Sheikh Mujib, the Friend of Bengal, was either writing impassioned articles and giving speeches to huge crowds, or was in jail on trumped-up charges, or in front of a court or, sometimes, was visiting his old friends, and drinking tea, and laughing as if nothing was happening to him, nothing at all.

6: How Big-uncle Left Home

1.

My father never got on with Laddu, my big-uncle, Boro-mama. And Boro-mama never liked my father. It was a difference of temperament, first, but their temperaments had led them to lead their lives in quite different ways. They were always going to fall out in a terrible way.

Of course, they were cousins before they were brothers-in-law. My father's mother was Nana's sister.

Boro-mama was not the eldest son. The eldest son had been killed in the Japanese air-raids during the war. Laddu was not used to the new burden of being eldest son when he and his sisters set off with Nana and Nani from Calcutta to Dacca, in 1947, and he probably never got used to it. His clever sister married their cousin, my father. But what was Boro-mama to do?

Boro-mama did not go on demonstrations in favour of the Bengali language. He did not end up in prison cells with intellectuals. When Dacca was burning with intellectual fervour and Tagore, Boro-mama was a plump boy of twenty, living at home with his mother and father without any occupation or interests.

Nana conspired to conceal this fact, and to keep his son Laddu busy with household tasks. Boro-mama was quite good with his hands, and it was surprising how many small jobs needed doing about the house. 'I noticed that the bath tap upstairs was dripping yesterday,' Nana said, over breakfast. 'If you have nothing else to do, you could see if it can be fixed.'

'It's probably the washer,' Boro-mama said knowledgeably.

'Well, perhaps you could mend it,' Nana said. 'If you have nothing else to do today.'

Round the breakfast table, Mary, Era, Nadira and Mira giggled at the thought that elder-brother might have anything else to do. Without a task, he would lie on the sofa from breakfast to dinner with his sandals off, listening to the radio or reading the newspaper. The nearest thing he had to action was to go out to the general store, where his neighbourhood cronies would sit all day long, deciding how they would improve the world over endless cups of tea. It was hilarious to his sisters that Laddu might have anything else to do. His youngest sister did not giggle: Dahlia sat in her high chair, looking from face to face with a cloth napkin about her chin, as her ayah spooned pap into her mouth. And his eldest sister did not giggle; my mother looked at her stern cousin, my father with a tie around his neck and a notebook and a frayed textbook by his plate, ready to go to his economics lectures at Dacca University. Neither of them saw this as very funny.

'No,' Boro-mama said slowly. 'I can do that this morning.'

So Nana set off to his chambers. Boro-mama's sisters, and his cousin, my father, went to university or to their different schools; Dahlia was carried off to her nursery. Boro-mama cut his newspaper-reading down to an hour or an hour and a quarter. He asked Nani for money for a cycle-rickshaw, and came back at the end of the morning with a small paper bag. After a cup of tea and some buns, he went in search of my grandfather's driver to borrow a small spanner from him; he returned in twenty minutes or slightly more. Finally, Boro-mama went upstairs and replaced the washer on the tap.

'There,' he said, coming down, glowing. 'That tap won't drip for years to come.'

Nani did not share Nana's view that it was better for Boro-mama to be doing small jobs around the house than nothing at all. She would have preferred it if Boro-mama had stayed at school until matriculation, and left with at least one or two qualifications. She also did not agree that Boro-mama's small occupations around the house would amount, in the end, to a life's work. She wondered who would ask Boro-mama to mend a tap if his father did not. So when Boro-mama announced, with an air of pride, that the tap he had fixed would not drip for years to come, she gave a small, tap-like sniff, and passed on.

When Nana came home from his chambers, Boro-mama announced the same thing.

'Excellent, excellent,' Nana said, rubbing his hands together. My father, coming in with Nana, with his notebook and textbook, made no comment. He went past to greet his cousin, my mother. They were in different faculties – my father in the economics faculty, and my mother in the political-science faculty. They often did not see each other all day between breakfast and their return.

'So that was one taka for the cycle-rickshaw to the ironmonger's,' Boro-mama said. 'And one for the washer – and I had to buy a new spanner, that was three more – and for the labour as

113

well . . .' He totted it up in his head, his eyes going to the ceiling, then to the floor, then all around the hallway. 'That makes seven taka,' he said eventually.

'That sounds about right,' Nana said, and took out three notes, which he handed to Boro-mama. Behind him, Nani, my father and my mother, who had been listening to this, walked away in silent indignation. As Nani was accustomed to say, Lord Curzon himself would come back to mend your tap, in person, if you paid him that much.

2.

Nana and Nani lived, in the 1950s, in a house in Rankin Street. It was a handsome, two-storey house, with plenty of room for them, their son and their four daughters. There was space, too, for other relations to come and live from time to time, for months or even years. The longest-term resident was, of course, my father.

My father had come to Dacca to study economics, and it was sensible for him to stay with his uncle, my Nana. Nana took it for granted that my father would live in a bedroom-cum-study for the whole of his course; he also took it for granted that one of his daughters would marry my father. Both these things happened. I doubt, however, that my father had any notion that he was fulfilling Nana's will by doing either of them, and if he had suspected it, he would have withdrawn immediately. As it happened, my mother and my father were great friends, and went together to a demonstration against the suppression of the Bengali language by the government. They were thrown into a prison cell together, with dozens of other protesters, and spent the night singing Bengali songs and shouting slogans. My father had grown up in a small village where his father was the teacher at the small mosque. The most exciting thing that had happened to him all his youth was catching a larger-than-usual fish out of a ditch with a twig, a string and a worm on a hook. Being thrown into jail was the most enjoyable night of my father's young life. In the morning, when he and my mother had been released, he went home with her, still singing Bengali songs about national rivers being dammed by the Pakistani yoke. He took a bath and put on a clean white shirt. He oiled and combed his hair. He grew sober. Then he went downstairs and asked my grandfather if he could marry my mother when he had graduated and had found a job in the government service. That would be some years in the future. My grandfather approved in general terms of a respectable young man who worked hard and could think of his life five years in the future, even of one who had spent the previous night in a prison cell.

Then he sent for my mother. He called her to his chambers in the court building, to make the matter as serious as he knew how. My mother walked nervously through the building's white Saracenic arches framing the arcades, each of the arches spattered at ground level with fans of red spit where paan-chewers had cleaned their mouths. Through the open doors, under slowly moving fans, men with great beards and sorrowful expressions draped themselves over ribbon-tied piles of paper in the dusty sunlight, like old bearded mothers in the nurseries where lawsuits are bred and weaned. My mother came finally to her father's chambers, and her father's boy asked her to wait, then showed her in, as if she were a client. My grandfather's methods worked almost too well. He said that her cousin Mahmood was a rascal who had no business taking her to demonstrations, and confined her to the house for the next ten days, sending her home in a rickshaw. My mother wept all through the rickshaw ride, not realizing that her future had been decided in accordance with her wishes.

The future of the household seemed obvious. The daughters, one by one, would grow up, take some education, marry and move out. There would be more sons-in-law like Mahmood, though probably not all of them cousins. There might even, in time, be more children for Nana and Nani. And Laddu would stay at home, taking care of the house, organizing repairs, rebuilding and repainting, perhaps some day taking responsibility for paying bills and supervising the gardeners, the driver, the household staff. Nana supported any number of dependants, hardly any of whom were related to him. There was no reason to suppose that Boro-mama would ever have a reason to leave the house.

3.

One day in the monsoon season, Nana came home from his chambers, and slipped on the wet leaves on the path in the front garden of Rankin Street. There was nothing remarkable about this, apart from the fact that Nana had also slipped on the wet leaves on his way out of the house in the morning. He came into the house with his hands smeared and muddy where he had fallen, calling out for a towel.

'I thought I asked somebody to clear the path,' he said, as he wiped his hands and threw the towel at Mary, who had brought it to him. That was his way: never to refer to demands made of Boro-mama, but just to say, 'I asked somebody'. 'Has the path been cleared?'

'The path?' Era said, coming out of the kitchen.

'No, Papa,' Mary said. 'I don't think it has.'

'That's really too much,' Nana said. 'Where is Laddu?'

There was a certain amount of household bustling in response. Era picked up Dahlia, who had toddled into the hallway to greet her father, and cluckingly carried her off. Mary suddenly found it very urgent to take the towel her father had used upstairs to the laundry basket. My mother and father were bewildered.

'Mira,' Nana said. 'Go and find your brother.'

'Your brother,' Era said. She looked immediately guilty, and walked quickly away upstairs.

Mira, only seven, watched her go with a puzzled expression. She did not know how to conceal a fact convincingly. 'I don't think elder-brother is here, Father,' she said.

'What is this?' Nana said, as my grandmother appeared. 'Where is he? He was supposed to carry out one small household chore – I simply asked him to sweep the garden path – and he hasn't done it. That really isn't like him at all.'

'No,' my grandmother said, though she certainly thought that failure to carry out a task to the end was very much like Boro-mama. 'I don't know where he is. I haven't seen him all day. Mira – where is Laddu?'

'I don't know,' Mira said, and then she burst into tears.

'What is this?' Nana said. 'Is this some kind of madhouse? Why won't anybody answer my question?'

'Ask – ask – ask –' Mira said, through her tears '– ask Era. She knows.'

'Era!' Nana shouted. 'Come back here!' My grandfather never shouted. It was one of the things his family admired about him. He never had to raise his voice to get his way. For years after-wards, the time when he shouted for Era-aunty was a favourite family story. The disappearance of Boro-mama was the only occasion when he really yelled. The family would recount this story, with amusement, and if anyone was there who did not know my grandfather, they would pause and look in puzzlement, wondering why it was a story that somebody should shout a name. 'Era!' my grandfather shouted. About him, everyone looked in wonderment, and Era came slowly out of the salon with the burden of what she knew.

'Me?' she said.

Of course it was Era who had been entrusted with the story. Era was a great reader of romantic fiction, and had cast her elder brother in the role of a Heathcliff, the man whom all the world is against, who has every disadvantage but who wins the beau-tiful heroine at last. Alone among her sisters, she actually looked up to Boro-mama. Even little Dahlia took him for granted, pummelling him and tugging her possessions rudely away from him, as if he were a nursery servant. Those long walks, those lengthy afternoons when Era and her brother were sequestered away, deep in conversation, they had discussed, it turned out, only one topic. Boro-mama loved to talk about himself; Era-aunty loved to listen and, no doubt, to echo the last thing he had said. He was wrong to think that she was a safe repository of secrets – as it turned out, she had been dropping hints to all of her sisters, apart from my mother, for weeks. They all knew where to point the finger on the day that my grandfather shouted. But she was the only one who had kept the entire story secret loyally.

'I think he has run off to marry Sharmin,' Era said, when they were all seated in the salon and some tea had been brought.

Nana looked at Nani, bewildered.

'You should never – never – have asked him to sweep the garden path,' she went on. 'That's why he's run away. You treat him like a servant. You would never ask Mahmood to sweep the garden path.' Era pointed dramatically at my father, punctilious in his white shirt and tie. 'You ask elder-brother to do all these things, and he does them without complaint. Just because he didn't go to university, like Mahmood.'

'But who is Sharmin?' Nana said.

Now it was Nani's turn to look shifty. 'I had no idea he was serious,' she said. And then the whole story came out.

Among Boro-mama's neighbourhood cronies was a man he had been to school with, Nawshad. Nawshad's family was not Bengali but Urdu-speaking: they came from Bihar. Nawshad was very much the same sort of wastrel as Boro-mama. He had grand schemes for making money – to open a cinema, to start importing American cigarettes into Dacca, to open a smart restaurant. None of these ever came to anything, because Nawshad had no money to invest, and none of the gang who spent their days smoking in the neighbourhood store had any money either.

Nawshad had a sister, however, called Sharmin. Sharmin was hard-working and academic, and was now studying at Mitford

Medical College. She would be a doctor in a year or two. No, she was not beautiful, but she was clever and interesting, and would get on in life.

She worked too hard, Nawshad said, and it was difficult to persuade her to go out, even to the cinema, once a month. But he did persuade her to come out to the cinema that Friday. It was a hot night, and wet; the cinema smelt of mould and bodies, and the film was an old one that broke down for ten minutes after the first reel. Sharmin had come out with her brother, and his friend Laddu had joined them. They had found plenty to talk about. He had made her laugh.

'Am I the only person in this family who didn't know about any of this?' Nana said.

It seemed that he was. Boro-mama had kept Era up to date with the details of their meetings, and their plans. Sharmin's family lived near Rankin Street, and were in fact known to Nana in general terms. Boro-mama had found opportunities to sneak out of the house and to meet Sharmin in quiet corners, underneath umbrellas, shaded by trees in the street, in the back corners of shops. It all sounded – to Era, and even retold bluntly when the story was over – terribly romantic. In time, Boro-mama had told Era that he wanted to marry Sharmin. He had asked her to explain the whole matter to their father.

'To Papa? I don't think I can, elder-brother,' Era said, alarmed. She had enjoyed the stories, and relished the monsoon-kisses, hopeless-doomed-passion aspect of her brother's life. But it had not occurred to her that the story might have possibilities for development. She had had noble renunciation in mind. It was not really credible to her that her brother would want to marry this Bihari girl, rather than take her tear-stained photograph from a secret drawer once a year, and kiss it.

'Well, I certainly can't,' Boro-mama said. 'He would throw me out of the house.'

'Why don't you ask Mahmood?' Era said. 'Papa likes him. He would make him listen.'

A dark expression passed over Boro-mama's features. 'I could never do that,' he said. 'I don't want to be in Mahmood's debt for anything.'

'In Mahmood's debt? Well,' Era said, quite briskly, 'I don't see anything else for it. You will just have to go and talk to Ma. If she can't explain it to Pa, then I don't think anyone will be able to.'

No one knew what the outcome was of the conversation between Boro-mama and his mother, the day when he told her that he wanted to marry an Urdu-speaking Bihari girl called Sharmin. Nobody even knew when or where it took place, this conversation. They were both at home in Rankin Street all day long, with nothing very much to occupy them. It was to be supposed that Boro-mama wandered into his mother's sitting room one morning and stayed there until the outcome was clear. Neither of them shared the details of the conversation with anyone else afterwards. Boro-mama told his sister Era about every detail of his courtship of Sharmin – the meetings under trees, the snatched five minutes, the outings to the park or the walks along the muddy Buriganga river with Nawshad, who knew to remove himself to a distance of fifteen yards. But when the conversation with Nani took place, nobody knew, nor what had been exchanged during it. Only when it was too late for anyone to do anything did it become clear that the conversation had taken place: that both of them had agreed never to mention anything about Sharmin, ever again; that Nani believed that whatever she had said had put an end to the whole business. She had seen no reason to mention any of it to my grandfather.

'Era,' my grandfather said, quite calmly, 'I am not going to punish you. Do you know when it was that Laddu decided to run away and marry this woman?'

Era looked about her helplessly; she gripped her pink scarf to her neck. 'I don't know when he decided,' she said.

'What I mean,' my grandfather said, in his most dispassionate and lawyerly way, 'is when was it that you knew for certain that he was going to run away?'

'To run away? Last night,' Era said. 'He told me last night that he was going to do it today. I should have told everyone. I could have stopped it altogether.'

'Very well,' my grandfather said. 'So I think we can all stop saying that Laddu ran away because I happened to ask him if he would see that the paths were cleared this morning. Clearly, he had made his decision before I mentioned that. Are we all agreed on that point?'

'Yes, Pa,' Mira, Mary, my mother and Era said, and Nana left the room.

'Am I in trouble?' Era said. 'I'm not going to be punished, Ma, am I?'

'Yes,' Nani said. 'You are in serious trouble. I am sure that when your father comes out of his chambers, he will tell me what your punishment is going to be.'

4.

For the next two years, nobody saw or heard of Boro-mama. The only fact that filtered back to Grandfather's house in Rankin Street was that he had, indeed, married a Bihari woman named Sharmin. Incomprehensibly, her family were as deeply opposed to her marriage as our family was. They did not see the apparent honour involved in her marrying Boro-mama, a man without profession, character or education, whose entire prospects had been torn away by the severing of relations with his father. 'I hope his father-in-law finds small jobs for him to do about the house,' my father said caustically. He had endured enough insults from Laddu about cuckoos in the nest, over-educated clowns worming their way into the bosoms of other people's fathers, and other mixed metaphors. He saw no reason to hold back when there was nobody but his cousins about.

Curiously, once Laddu had left the house, my father did not

121

find it a more comfortable berth. It might have been thought that, with the departure of his only male cousin, my father would find life in Rankin Street very easy. My aunts were fond of their cousin, in general terms, although they did not pretend to understand the esteem in which my mother held him; my grandfather greatly respected him, and was forever holding him up as an example of hard work, discipline and moral rectitude to anyone who would listen and to a few who would not. But perhaps my grandfather needed to berate somebody; perhaps my father feared that he would soon find himself being given the sorts of household tasks that Boro-mama had found so profitable. I don't know this for sure, but perhaps once – just once – Nana asked my father if he could possibly spare the time from his economics studies to have a look at the tap that seemed to be dripping in the downstairs bathroom.

My father was an independent-minded sort of person. Two months after Boro-mama's sudden departure, and a couple of weeks after news had reached Rankin Street that he was irrevocably married to a woman who barely spoke Bengali, my father had moved out too, to a university hall. The gossips exaggerated: Sharmin, even then, spoke perfectly serviceable Bengali, though it was not her first language.

In the next two years, my father finished his economics degree, and then his MA in the same subject. He applied for the government service, and finished almost at the top of his cohort. He was appointed to a job as assistant district commissioner in Barisal, a middle-sized town twelve hours' journey by rocket launch from Dacca. It was decided between him and my mother that they could get married in the middle of 1959. My grandfather and grandmother were very pleased. There seemed no reason to think that Mahmood would disappear from their lives in the way that Boro-mama had done.

During the British time, a space had been cleared in Dacca for a park. It was not made by the British, but it nevertheless had the air of pallid pleasure of the sort that the British enjoyed so much. It was called Balda Garden. As often with the British, it had an educational, almost museum quality. There were collections of botanical specimens from all over the world, some in the open air and some in a few rather crumbling hothouses. There were lawns and flowerbeds, and to that the British had added their own rather limp notions of enjoyment – a lake that had perhaps once been intended for boating parties, but was now just a kidney-shaped lake, and a picturesque Joy House, a combination of Swiss rest-house and Greek amphitheatre to one side. These joyless festival sites had now been taken over and colonized by my nation and its sense of fun. Constant supervision could keep Bengalis on their best behaviour for only so long. There were vendors of sweets and of tea; there were large families spread out comfortably on the lawns; there were picnics that took an entire afternoon to reach the end of; there were balloon-sellers and even, once, an acrobat. Under the trees, where it was quiet and shady, couples sat in peace and quiet, feeding each other from their picnic boxes, blushing, and laughing under their breath. It was a favourite place to visit on a Sunday, which was then the day of rest and pleasure in Dacca, as Friday is now.

My mother and father, before their marriage, regularly met at the Joy House on a Sunday evening. They would walk around the park, talking in the sort of privacy you can only have on the street or in crowds in Dacca.

Both of them were highly punctual people, and when they agreed to meet at the Joy House at six, both of them would be there at six. My father, however, was still more punctual than my mother – in fact, he often regarded her as a poor time-keeper. This was unfair, since she generally arrived at the time specified; my father would arrive a good fifteen or twenty minutes in advance, and pace up and down, inspecting his watch.

At twenty to six, my father was already standing at the Joy House, waiting impatiently. It was a favourite place for meetings, and he stood among people who had made arrangements to meet at half past five as well as a few early arrivals for six, like himself. Along the path came couples, families and small groups of young men, out for a Sunday-afternoon walk. The sun was in my father's eyes, and the groups approaching from his left were mere silhouettes. When a figure greeted him, hesitantly, my father did not know immediately who it was, and greeted him back without hesitation. When he realized that it was Laddu, who would not have realized that my father was standing in a blinding light, it was too late to withdraw the greeting.

'We often come here,' Laddu said. 'It is so pleasant. I wonder – could I introduce my wife to you?'

Boro-mama's wife was, it appeared, the small, sweet, round person by his side. She was not a beauty, but had a pleasant, open face and pale, rather yellowish colouring. Her name was Sharmin, and my father greeted her politely. In the heat, the pre-monsoon congestion in the air, she fanned herself with curt and efficient gestures. Boro-mama asked after everyone, and was surprised to learn that my father no longer lived at the house in Rankin Street. My father thought that Laddu gave him a look of near-respect on hearing this. Like many habitual dependants, Boro-mama made a point of denouncing and disapproving of other people's sponging, as he often called it.

They talked, quite cheerfully, for ten minutes, until my father mentioned that he was waiting for my mother. A look of doubt crossed Boro-mama's face, and he seemed almost on the verge of running away. 'Oh, Laddu,' Sharmin said, taking hold of his arm. To my father's surprise, Laddu suggested that they meet later in the week, perhaps to see a film. My father said – I am sure he said – that he was very busy with work, and with preparations to go to Barisal to take up his post as assistant district commissioner. But Boro-mama pressed him, and eventually he agreed. It was five to six: Boro-mama and Sharmin said their goodbyes and left. It was obvious that they would not risk an encounter with my mother, or with any of the rest of Laddu's family, just yet.

5.

The night after my father and Laddu went to the cinema together, my father was invited round to Nana's house to have dinner. He had a regular weekly evening there as the guest of my mother. While he was waiting to take up his appointment in Barisal, my father had continued living in the university residence. It had its disadvantages. The price he paid for the independence of living there was perpetual hunger. In the residence, food was provided as part of the living expenses. But there were hundreds of other hungry young economists living in the same place, and the food was basic, dull and prepared in great vats. Like all male students, at any time, at any place, my father was appallingly hungry from one end of the week to the other. His evening at Nana's would set him up for the barren remainder of the week, eking out the institution's thin dal and rice, the meagre pickings of its birianis with memories of Nana's dinner and the occasional bought treat. He was punctilious about waiting for an invitation, and would not have come if he were not asked; fortunately, my mother was just as punctilious about asking him, once a week.

The monsoon rains had broken that week. My father, the aunts and Nani sat inside the house, looking out on the veranda. The garden was already soaked with mud; the rains made a deep, resonant trill on the flat surfaces of the house, made the trees spatter and slap. Because of the sound of the rain, nobody heard Nana's car approaching, and the first anyone knew of him was his voice in the hall. 'Is nobody here?' he called, and then they heard his umbrella being rapidly opened and shut, two or three times. His daughters came out to the hall to meet him behind Nani; my father following somewhere in the back.

'What is that sound?' Nana said, after he had greeted them all and handed his raincoat and umbrella to the boy.

'What sound?' Nani said.

'That sound of dripping,' he said. 'It kept me awake all last night. Can you hear?'

The aunts compared notes, discovered that they could not hear any particular dripping. Mira asked if he meant the sound of the rain on the terrace, and was asked if she thought he was a fool, and not to be so pert, child.

'I asked for something to be done about it,' Nana said. 'I distinctly asked for something to be done.'

Nani asked, and it became clear that my grandfather was talking about the tap in the upstairs bathroom. It had started dripping the day before. My grandfather could not endure the sound of a dripping tap in the house, and in the end, he said, he had got up in the middle of the night and placed a towel in the hand-basin to mute the sound. As was his way, he must have said, as he left the house in the morning, 'Somebody ought to do something about that dripping tap.' What had happened was that the towel had been removed from the basin, and nothing else had been attempted. My grandfather gave my father, as the only other man in the house, a long, assessing, unfair look, as if he had been there to overhear the suggestion in the morning, and should have done something about the dripping tap. My father looked back.

Once they were seated at table, and my father's first brutish hunger had been satisfied – my mother's sisters used to watch him, stifling giggles, as he laid into the mutton curry – he sat back in his chair and began a conversation.

'It is interesting, this new film,' he said.

'What film are you talking about, Mahmood?' my mother said. He was not a great cinema-goer. Normally he barely listened when my mother's sisters talked about a film they had seen, or some other entertainment.

'There is a film in the cinemas that was shot near Dacca, on the delta,' he said, in a measured way. He stretched his neck, rotated his shoulders, took another mouthful of curry.

It was like my father to assume that nobody else could have known about this film. It had been discussed during its filming by the intelligentsia. A film-maker had gone into the delta and shot the ordinary people at their tasks of fishing and working. It had been said in advance that this would herald a new age of film-making in the region. But *Jago Hua Savera* had come out and nobody had gone to see it at all. Apart from my grandfather, who referred to the cinema scornfully as 'the flicks', everyone in the family was a keen film-goer. But in this case, Era and Mira had gone to see it and returned with big yawns, saying that they had never suffered so much in their lives as at the hands of *Jago Hua Savera* and its fisherfolk.

'Yes,' my father said. 'It is an interesting film.'

'Did you stay to the end, Mahmood?' Era said.

'Yes,' my father said. 'I stayed to the end.' My mother took a large spoonful of rice, poised it above his plate, gave it a good shake, and then offered him a bowl of dal. 'It is only playing in one cinema, I believe.'

'Which cinema is that, Mahmood?' my grandfather said.

'The Shabistan,' my father said. 'It is a very old cinema.'

'I never saw a film as wonderful as *Pyaasa*,' my grandmother said. 'Did you see *Pyaasa*, Mahmood?'

'Oh, yes, *Pyaasa*, that was a film,' Era said. She started singing at the dinner table, a thing my grandfather utterly detested. 'And so sad! One could have cried.'

My grandmother and aunts started comparing their favourite scenes in *Pyaasa*, a film that had taken Dacca by storm two years ago, and was still being talked about. Probably there were cinemas, even then, which were still playing it to faithful audiences. When they had finished, my father said, 'That sounds quite different from *Jago Hua Savera*. I liked it, but Laddu found it dull, just as you did, Era.'

'Who found it dull, Mahmood?' my grandfather said.

'Laddu,' my father said.

'Laddu, did you say?' my grandmother said.

My father went on to explain – he had the attention of the table now. There was no question that not all his sisters-in-law-to-be

127

held him in the great esteem that my mother did, and my grandfather did. For some of them, he was a not very exciting country cousin who, by means of hard work and honesty, had made his way in the world, and was to be the man their eldest sister would marry. They were not rude to him, but they were not accustomed to give him their full attention at the dinner table. They had never spent a night with him in the police cells, singing songs of resistance and independence, and had always found it tricky to visualize the story when my mother told it to them, as she quite frequently did. But once or twice in his life, my father successfully dropped a bombshell, and made people listen to what he had to say. This was one of those times. The whole family listened to him, explaining that he had met not just Laddu, but Laddu's wife Sharmin. At first by chance, in the Balda Gardens, by the Joy House, but afterwards by arrangement: the three of them had gone to see *Jago Hua Savera* only the day before.

'You met her, Mahmood?' Mira said. 'What is she like?'

'Laddu was full of plans,' my father said. 'He kept talking about the cinema, all through the film – he kept saying that nobody had done anything to this cinema for years except change its name. He kept saying that if he had some money, he could run the cinema, transform it into a wonderful place, that it could hardly fail. I don't think the film really held his attention. But I enjoyed it.'

'But what is she like?' Mary said. 'Is she tall or short, fat, thin, is she pretty?'

'I wouldn't say she was pretty,' my father said. 'Not pretty, exactly. But there is something quite agreeable about her face.'

There was a long pause; the whole table sat waiting for my father to continue, but he just went on eating. That seemed to be all he had observed about Laddu's wife.

'And is she sensible, or is she a fool?' Nani said finally. 'How could she marry Laddu in such a hole-and-corner way?'

'I don't know,' my father said. 'We didn't go into all that.'

'I suppose we could ask Laddu and his wife to come here for

dinner,' my grandfather said. 'It seems ridiculous never to see him. And I should meet his wife, before she decides to give us grandchildren. Yes, on the whole, I think Mahmood is right. We should ask Laddu and his wife round here for dinner next week. Not next week – ask them to come as soon as they may. Tomorrow. Push the boat out.'

My father had not, in fact, suggested asking Laddu and Sharmin round for dinner at all. But my grandfather was thinking about the dripping tap in the bathroom next to his bedroom.

7: Nana's Faith in Rustum

1.

In the autumn of 1959, my father and mother married in Dacca. Immediately after their marriage, they went to Barisal, where my father took up his government post as an assistant district commissioner.

There is a large album of photographs of their wedding; formal, well mounted, in a solid volume. Nana used to collect the albums of all his children's weddings, a long line of them in the sitting room; nowadays, I believe my sister has them. In one of the photographs, my mother sits among her sisters. They are solemn-faced: being photographed was still a novelty in the 1950s. The photographs, now, do not seem very festive to us. People lined up and faced the camera. Still, in their lovely pale saris and their wide eyes against the dark wall, my mother and her sisters look like a floating grove of water-lilies. Nani, to one side, still looks young; interested; responsible. I never thought of her as beautiful in her old age, when I knew her, or as one of those women of whom one says, 'How beautiful she must have been when she was young.' But here, just short of fifty, surrounded by her daughters and one son, with one white streak in her hair, just that, she seems at the confident peak of her looks and health. The bright-eyed boy at her feet, her competent hand resting on his head, is Pultoo; the baby in her arms must be Bubbly-aunty. And my mother? Well, that is just my mother. My aunts and the rest of the family may have called her Shiri, but to me she will always be just my mother. The photographs of my father, with his father, his father-in-law, and other male relations seem by comparison tense and wary; my father has somehow been pushed unwillingly to the front of the picture, where he would rather not be. Both sets of photographs seem posed, but only my aunts give the impression that they have been looking forward to posing for the photographer.

They are very different from the photographs of my wedding, as I suppose my wedding was very different from my parents'. Among my wedding photographs, there are images of my new husband feeding me cake; of some rather drunk guests dancing in globes of disco-lighting; of serried ranks of canapés waiting for the party to begin; of many other things that did not happen at my parents' wedding, exactly fifty years before mine, and many things, including the fact of my wedding itself, which were not thought of in 1959, in a country that did not yet exist. But my parents' wedding was a happy day.

Somewhere in the picture of my father with his male relations there is the dark face of Boro-mama, Big-uncle. My grandfather had sent Laddu and his new wife Sharmin an invitation. It had been discovered, after my father had made an approach to them, that the two were living with Sharmin's sister while Sharmin completed her medical degree. Nani was indignant that her eldest son had, apparently, absconded from her house, not to make his own way in life but to go to live off somebody else; not even his wife, since she was studying, but his wife's sister, of whom nothing was known. She kept her comments to herself, and to her daughters, her women friends and neighbours; Nana, who may have thought some of the same things, said nothing what-ever against Laddu's domestic circumstances. My parents' wedding would be the perfect opportunity for Laddu to intro-duce his new wife into the family circle, and to allow himself to be forgiven.

Laddu apologized, but his wife Sharmin was expecting a child, and would not be able to come. However, he was happy to come.

Looking at the photograph, in which Boro-mama stands in a charcoal suit between grandfathers, I try to distinguish some awkwardness, resentment or embarrassment in his face. But he has exactly the same formal, sober, puzzled expression that every Bengali seems to have assumed whenever he was faced with a camera in the 1950s.

2.

After the wedding, my mother and father travelled to Barisal, and my father began his professional life.

The experience was harder for my mother than for my father. My father had grown up in the country. He was used to a quiet existence, and an unsophisticated one. He did not mind a small circle of acquaintances, and did not long for novelty or excitement. He had, too, while studying in Dacca, learnt about self-reliance. These were the characteristics that my mother had admired in her cousin when she agreed to marry him. She was the least extrovert of her sisters, and had never thought of herself as the product of a big city, fashionable or forward in any way. But when she found herself living in a district like Barisal, she discovered that she had, after all, the imprint of some metropolitan habits.

Barisal was a port town, sleepy and remote. Much of it was built of red brick, flushed and rather angry-looking; the largest building in the city was the post office, a palace of almost military grandeur, which in more important towns the British would have faced with marble. The estuary front was busy with rusting launches and fishing boats, coming to and fro, puffing black smoke into the air, the water made slick by their discharges of oil. The ferry port was a constant host to those families, their luggage piled up like great clusters of grapes on the quayside, who are always and will always be transporting themselves from one side of Bengal to the other, as long as Bengal exists. There was something greasy and rusting about the whole town.

In those days, you travelled by rocket launch from Dacca. The government accommodation provided for assistant district commissioners was furnished, so my mother and father travelled with only a few things to begin their married life. A case, between a suitcase and a trunk in size, took my mother's clothing – she knew she would never be able to buy good-quality silk in a place like Barisal – with a box of jewellery buried deep inside. Another case held their books – they had packed separately, but Mahmood had left his books at Nana's house when he moved out, so it seemed sensible to combine his small professional library with my mother's books, a few novels and anthologies of poetry, and pack them all together. My father's clothes and possessions filled a single brown suitcase, and on top of the pile on the back of the porter's wagon, lumbering towards the port and the rocket launch that would take them to their new home in Barisal, was my grandparents' wedding gift: a fine pier-glass in a gold frame, wrapped in layers of cardboard to survive the journey. Other gifts, such as the dining table and chairs, which the uncles had clubbed together to provide, had stayed in Dacca for the time being. Nobody thought that my mother and father would remain in a place like Barisal for very long.

The area was remote and rudimentary. There were, it was said, tigers still roaming the countryside, and one nearby had taken a villager only months before. My mother had only ever seen a tiger in the Calcutta zoo. Many towns in the district were cut off by road from civilization for weeks on end during the rainy season. As the roads that ran along ridges between paddy-fields could be washed away, even when the waters receded there could remain weeks more of isolation while they were rebuilt. Of course, as my father said, during the rainy season, Dacca was often cut off as well. My mother wondered what Dacca was cut off from. It seemed quite sufficient in itself. Whether it was raining or not, Barisal seemed far away and strange, connected only by the water that, for much of the year, isolated other settlements. Shiri regularly thought, during the three years she and my father spent in Barisal, of the heroines of Chekhov, longing for Moscow: he was a writer she had often read without ever quite understanding before.

My mother had expected to live more simply in Barisal than she had in her father's house in Rankin Street. When the porters drew up in front of the ill-kept red-brick bungalow in a line of similar bungalows, however, she realized she had made a mistake in her mind. Her notion of simplicity was of a quality opposed to ornateness or, she realized, the processes of accretion, which had happened in her father's house. Despite moves, war and forced emigration, her father's house had comfortably acquired possessions, furniture, adornments in large numbers. But so, too, it seemed, had the furnished semi-detached bungalow. The caretaker, once found and hailed by the carter, let them in, and the pair of them carried in their three cases.

Once the cases had been deposited in the hallway, and the brownish, flickering electric light had been turned on, it was clear that no preparations had been made for a newly-wed couple. The house was filled with furniture – the rejected, colossal mahogany sideboards, caryatid-supported sofas and tallboys, polished brown and malevolent as giant horrid beetles – that had been out of fashion for forty years at least. Every piece would, on its own, have been too large for the modest rooms; three or four of the hardwood behemoths made an impassable labyrinth. The sad, unchosen selection was very different from her father's warm, mismatched rooms. In the weeks to come, they would discover that the bungalow had been left uninhabited for a year and a half. It had slowly become the repository, among all their neighbours, of any inherited furniture, perfectly good in itself but no longer needed, especially those pieces of giant furniture, which had an aura of evil, rendered in mahogany. Mahmood had lived very simply, with no real attention to comfort or elegance, all his life. But even he seemed dismayed by the bungalow; even he could tell the difference between the warm, damp garden smell of his father-in-law's house, with its easy comfort and soothing lights, and this low, dank place, green mould covering half the back wall and sharp carved mahogany ornamentation, deliberately barking your shins at every turn.

The next morning Shiri woke, and went in the early-morning light through her overcrowded rooms. Outside, in what she thought was her garden, a man was squatting, folded up like a fan, gazing down the muddy road as if at the dawn, waiting for something to happen.

The neighbours soon made themselves known. Like Mahmood, they all worked for the government in Islamabad, filing reports in Urdu and supplying information at their remote superiors' requests. There was little variety. Shiri had never had much of a taste for society; her social life was led among her sisters, a few friends and the daughters of neighbours. In her family, she was a byword for her reluctance to leave home and pay a call. She had never loved the passing of compliments over the tea table and, before her marriage, had never felt concern that Mahmood might deprive her of her very ordinary social life.

But, very soon, she felt first a vague dissatisfaction and then a positive dismay at the limits of the world in which she found herself. Around her was no social variety but the families of her husband's new colleagues. They had come to Barisal from all parts of Pakistan – not just from the Bengali-speaking side, from Dacca and the surrounding provinces, but some, too, from the Urdu-speaking part of the country, the western segment. The men had been posted here, and brought their families. Those families, living for the most part in the bungalows around, were the only society to be had. It did not seem possible to gain access to people who had been born, had grown up and remained in Barisal. And so my mother, who had never felt addicted to social variety, found herself in a world too restricted even for her.

At tea parties, among the mothers and wives of Mahmood's

colleagues, Shiri sat quietly. 'We have had to let our girl go,' one woman said. 'When I counted the sacks of rice, she had been feeding her whole family on our supplies for months.'

'They are so dishonest,' another woman, a Pakistani, said, 'these people. One took an entire bag of chillies – he thought I would not notice. It is really extraordinary.'

Shiri thought she would contribute. 'At home,' she said, 'my friend is great friends with Sheikh Mujib's daughter, Hasina, and she tells a story about a tremendous fuss Hasina made once about the very same thing. She was expecting fifteen sacks of chilli from their estate, and what arrived were only thirteen. She made such a fuss – as if she did not have other things to interest herself in than two missing sacks of chilli.'

But there was a shuffling, an inspection, and a moving on. What was it? Did they not know who Sheikh Mujib was? Did they think there was nothing so very funny in a complaint about servants' honesty? Shiri looked about her, at the young mothers and wives, three of them pregnant; she heard herself beginning to tell the story again, but this time as a story of motherhood, disloyal servants, and the difficulties of living in Barisal. She had not married Mahmood for this.

My father had got to know his colleagues first and, when he returned home at night, he was able to tell her the names and habits of those colleagues. It was like an interesting story to his new wife. And as the weeks passed, she found herself meeting the families of the people that Mahmood had talked about and, in the end, meeting them at home, or in their homes. But now she had got there, everything seemed so hierarchical, and she had to learn who could invite whom first. But in time she got the hang of it, just as the walls were scrubbed and repainted, and most of the furniture cleared out. She and my father made a go of it. It would not be for ever. Four months after they had moved to Barisal, my mother was pregnant. It would be with my elder brother, Zahid.

3.

Even in 1960 it was possible to write a letter from Barisal to Dacca. It was not a swift process. To travel there oneself meant a long journey in rusty old ferries. Even with the best organization and a purposeful will, it would take days rather than hours. And the same was true of a letter, which in any case had to travel in precisely the same way.

When the letter from my mother to Nani turned up in Rankin Street, probably nobody considered how it had had to travel. If they had thought of the ferry, and the heavy plummeting and plunging of its journey, the request would not have been made; the answer would have been different. There was, too, the question of travelling along the roads of the town, in vehicles that probably had iron-rimmed wheels. It was reckless of my mother to think of travelling over such roads in such a way while pregnant. But in the end all was well: my brother Zahid was born at the normal time. Life is full of such decisions, and turns that come to no harm; moments of normality, where no story springs and nothing goes wrong.

The letters were laid out on my grandfather's desk each morning. My grandmother liked to go through them, and separate them into correspondence from clients, and personal family letters. The letters came in one bundle, and Grandmother had to pick out her private correspondence from the general pile. That morning's pile included my mother's weekly letter: she was a punctual correspondent.

My grandmother opened the letter at the desk with the creamy old ivory paperknife, and stood in the study, reading in the slatted light. Alone, she smiled, smoothed out the page on the green leather surface of the desk; she let herself be alone with the knowledge for just one moment. Her other daughters were downstairs: Mary was minding little Bubbly; Era and Mira could be heard talking quietly, intermittently – they were both reading and passing comments as they went.

My grandmother opened the study door carefully. Her chappals clapped against her feet as she carefully went downstairs. She measured her tread. There was no reason to hurry with her news. In the salon, playing with little Bubbly, along with Mary, was Laddu's wife Sharmin. When she did not have classes, she quite often came round to her mother-in-law's house, these days. She made herself useful, and welcome.

'There is a letter from Shiri, from Barisal,' Nani said, to the room in general. 'She says she is having a baby.'

'Shiri, a mother,' Mira said, jumping up and dropping her work on the floor. 'She was only married six months ago. How can someone have a baby when she is only just married?'

'Just married! Don't be such a baby yourself,' Era said, setting her book down. 'Such exciting news. Is Mahmood excited too?'

'It is so strange to think of them being mother and father,' Nadira said. She had been upstairs, and had followed her mother down; she stood, posing, at the foot of the stairs, her arm outstretched along the banister. 'They will be so strict. What clever, dark little babies they are going to have. Sharmin, you have never met my sister Shiri. You don't know what they are like. I can't imagine her having a baby.'

'No,' Sharmin said. She had a charming, unusual accent; it had made her sisters-in-law smile at first, and then, of course, it was just Sharmin's way of talking. 'No, I have never met her. But of course I have heard you all talk about her, and I have met Mahmood. I know what he is like. I would have thought that he would make a very good father, Nadira. Do you think that you are going to make a good aunt?' She heaved herself upwards; she herself was heavily pregnant, and her own confinement could only be days or weeks away.

Nadira's eyes grew big. Taking small, graceful, half-running steps, she went to the mirror in the hallway to inspect herself. 'I had not thought of that,' she said. 'Me – an aunt.'

'But you will be an aunt,' my grandmother said. 'And so will Mira, and so will Dahlia, and even baby Bubbly will be an aunt.'

'How can Bubbly be anyone's aunt?' Nadira said. 'She is only just born herself. She can hardly walk. She is no use to anyone. How can she possibly be allowed to be an aunt?'

'Nevertheless,' Nani said, 'she is going to be the baby's aunt. Now, are you going to sit quietly and listen to what else your sister has to say in her letter?'

It may seem strange that my aunts grew excited at the news that they were about to become aunts at the birth of my brother when, by their side, their sister-in-law was also heavily pregnant. They were not being rude. The reason for this was that in Bengali, there is one word for an aunt of a brother's child – the aunt of Laddu's son, who when he was born was called Ejaj – and there is another word for the aunt of your sister's child, such as my brother Zahid, whose impending birth was causing so much excitement (khala and fupu). And, of course, to be the aunt of Sharmin's child was quite a different excitement and a different name altogether, which had been got over with and forgotten about. We like to have as many family excitements as possible, we Bengalis.

My grandmother read the letter out loud. In it, my mother complained rather about Barisal; she said that she did not much like the house they were in, which she had said before, and that Mahmood was getting on well at work with his colleagues, where he was much respected, but that it was difficult to find good servants and that the arguments with the cook had continued, and they had had to find a new maid-of-all-work when the old one had proved dirty. (The cook had turned out to be the master of only three dishes, which came about with terrible monotony, and resisted any suggestion from my mother about a fourth dish – her eventual departure in a rage, an hour before my father's superior and his wife arrived for dinner, was another of my mother's few stories of their life in Barisal. Not that the cook's three dishes were very delicious – the food, my mother said, in Barisal, was simply inedible.) None of these complaints was new. Still, she went on, with all these difficulties, they did have some good news, which she would not hold back from them further: she and Mahmood were to have a baby, in six months' time. And this was fresh to my mother's sisters.

('You see?' Era said to Mira. 'She is not having her baby now. It is coming in six months' time. Now do you understand?'

'Yes, I think I understand,' Mira said.)

They were very happy at this news, my mother wrote, but it was impossible to imagine having the baby in Barisal. The facilities were so wretched, the local doctor old and ignorant and set in his ways. And my mother could not imagine having her first baby without her mother and father and sisters around.

'Sharmin, do you think . . . ?' my grandmother said.

'I think,' Sharmin said slowly, 'I think she might not exaggerate. Some of these country doctors! And perhaps the hospital in Barisal has not been renovated since the British time – since it was built, even. I am afraid that the government in Karachi does not always think of hospitals in East Pakistan when they have money to spend on improving matters. Sometimes mothers-to-be worry needlessly. There is no doubt about that. For myself' – she gestured downwards generally – 'I would not want to have my baby in Barisal.'

'Well, that is just what Shiri says,' my grandmother said.

'I could very easily look up the mother-and-child mortality rates in Barisal,' Sharmin said.

There was a general sucking of teeth, and Mary even made a warding-off sign. Sharmin was a practical, intelligent scientist: she sometimes forgot that she was not talking to other practical, intelligent scientists, but to my aunts.

'Shiri is in no doubt,' my grandmother said. 'She is going to come back and live here before the baby is born. So that is settled. She says that Mahmood will come when the baby is born, and then go back to Barisal, and she and the baby will go back and join them later. I wonder what they will call the dear dark little thing? I am sure it is going to be terribly clever. It will be doing sums in its crib.'

And that was insightful and prophetic of my grandmother, because, indeed, my brother Zahid was to grow up to be a scientist, and to be famous in the family for being able to do very complicated long division in his head before he was ten, and for asking his teachers if they could give him some more sums and equations to do, and sucking his pencil sagely, and for explaining to Nani how she should find out the height of the tamarind tree in front of her house with a protractor and a piece of weighted string, and so on and so forth in the way of very clever children of clever parents, which my parents certainly were.

'A very clever baby, however dark it is going to be. Once Shiri comes back to Dacca,' Era said, 'she is never going to go back to Barisal. She will make Mahmood come and work in Dacca, too. She loves the bright lights too much.'

At this absurdity of Era's, all her sisters giggled behind their hands until Sharmin, who had never met my mother, had to ask what was so amusing. My mother was certainly a modern, capable

141

person, who took charge of business. In that sense she was the product of a city. But she was not someone who could be thought of as loving the bright lights, as Era put it. However, Era was right in her diagnosis, and after the birth of my brother, Ma only briefly went back to Barisal, and for ever afterwards talked about it with a shudder. At six months pregnant, she endured the rattle and shake of the journey back home on those terrible rust-and-steel launches, banging along the rivers like empty biscuit tins, the stench of their black smoke and the foul stink of the water as the boat ran by the tanneries turning her green and making her puke discreetly into a bucket constantly for twenty hours. But, in the event, no harm came to her or to my brother Zahid.

4.

I know what the wooing-and-courtship-and-engagement of my mother and father was like: it must have been very much like the way they behaved to each other when they had been married for decades. They never lost the air of formal respect for each other. My mother had respect for my father because he was so hard-working and ambitious a man. When he attained his ambitions, it did not increase her respect, since she had always had trust in him. My father had respect for my mother because of whose daughter she was: he always felt himself, to some degree, the poor cousin. To the end of their lives, they never used affectionate names for each other. They always addressed each other with the word 'you'.

But I do not know what the wooing-and-courtship-and-engagement of Boro-mama and Sharmin was like. It was carried on away from the eyes of his family, and of hers; under umbrellas, in the rain, during walks in the public gardens and in cinemas, where they would arrive separately and then sit together. They married in secret, and went to live with Sharmin's sister, whom none of us ever really knew, while Sharmin was finishing her medical degree. So I do not know what they were like at the beginning of their marriage either. All I know is what they were like when my mother returned from Barisal.

'Sometimes a baby is born with two heads,' Nadira said, in the salon at Rankin Street.

'That must be useful,' Dahlia said.

'Useful, how?' Sharmin said. She hooked her fingers underneath the blouse of her sari, tugged and straightened, pulled a swatch of loose sari material, the anchal, as we call it, across her belly. All her sisters-in-law were there, apart from Bubbly, who was having her afternoon nap upstairs. 'How can it be useful to have two heads?'

'You could use one to look forward, and the other to look back,' Nadira said. 'Or you could talk with one head and read with the other one. Or, in the train, you could look out of the window and read the map at the same time. It would be wonderful to have two heads.'

'Your baby is going to be so lucky,' Era said.

'Lucky, how?' Sharmin said.

'Why, if it is born with two heads,' Nadira said, straightfacedly, 'it would really be a gift, if you think about it.'

'We saw a calf born with two heads,' Dahlia said, meaning herself and Nadira. 'It was in the village. Nobody thought that was very useful. They killed it.'

'Pay attention, now,' Mira said to Dahlia seriously. They were both sitting on the sofa, Mira showing Dahlia a stitching trick in needlework. 'Look – you see, I make a kind of loop here, and leave it, not too tight-tight, not too slack, and then – ah – yes. That's it. You see? Now you try.'

'That's right,' Nadira said. 'They did kill it, didn't they? But nobody would kill a dear little baby just because it had two heads.'

'My baby isn't going to have two heads,' Sharmin said composedly. 'Of that I can be sure.'

'Stranger things have happened,' Mary said. 'There is a picture

143

in the encyclopedia of the famous Siamese twins. They were born linked together, at the chest, and they married a pair of sisters and died within three hours of each other at the end of a long life.'

'The end of two long lives, you mean,' Nadira said.

'The end of two long lives, I suppose,' Mary said. 'Well, they had two heads.'

'Two heads? But that is not the same, Mary,' Dahlia said. 'I don't think you quite understand. Those were twins who were joined together. They had two bodies as well as two heads. That is not the same thing at all as Sharmin's baby, if it is born with two heads. That is more like the calf in the village that had to be killed.'

'Babies are never born with two heads,' Sharmin said, without raising her voice. 'Or hardly ever. And I am sure that my baby is not going to be born with two heads.'

'Well,' Nadira said, 'it would be awfully sad if that happened.' And she cast a dramatic sigh. She got up, a graceful, glowing twelve-year-old in a floral, aquamarine cotton frock with puffed sleeves, and went over to the harmonium. She doodled a few notes, then sang a few more. She had a sweet, tuneful voice: her father, in company, would often ask her to perform, her sisters more rarely.

'Sing the song about the flower,' Era said. Nadira ignored her, doodling on the keyboard and singing in a half-voice, as if thinking through the music.

'The thing about a baby – an *unusual* baby –' Nadira said.

'Stop teasing poor Sharmin,' Mira said. She had been occupied, her head down over the embroidery, letting Dahlia follow the sequence of steps with the needle and the bobbin, wrapped tightly with pale blue thread. 'Really, Nadira – stop it. There will be no baby with two heads. Sharmin's baby will be simply perfect, you wait and see.'

'Simply perfect,' Dahlia echoed.

Nadira turned round from the harmonium, breaking off her song. 'But very pale. Look how pale Sharmin is, even sitting next to Era.'

'Yes, she's sitting next to me, and still looks pale, it's true,' Era said complacently. 'Until Sharmin came, I really was the palest of everyone. It must be so strange, everyone in West Pakistan being so pale, even paler than I am.'

'And Laddu has always been dark,' Mary said. 'Mama thought he was a monster when he was born, she told me once.'

'But he's very handsome now,' Mira said.

Era patted Sharmin's arm encouragingly. 'Even if he is dark. No one thought he was a monster.'

'But, Mira,' Dahlia said, 'you weren't there at the time. How could you possibly know?'

'Yes, they will have such dark little babies,' Nadira said. 'They will take after Laddu, I am sure of it. Such dear, dear, black little babies.'

'That's enough,' Mary said, looking up; she pulled the thread tight, held it up to her teeth, and bit to sever it. 'Sharmin, don't listen to them. They are all very silly and rude.'

'Oh, I don't mind,' Sharmin said. 'And it may well be true – Laddu is dark, and we say, you know, that the first baby takes after its father, and if it is a boy, it takes still more after its father. So the baby is bound to be dark, poor little thing. Dark babies are always full of energy, and I know this one will be – I can feel him kicking me all the time.'

'Doesn't that feel strange?' Dahlia said. 'A little stranger kicking you from the inside?'

'We can kick you from the outside, if you want to know what it feels like,' Nadira said. 'There is no problem whatsoever about that.'

5.

My father stayed in Rankin Street until my brother Zahid was born. He was born upstairs, in my grandparents' bedroom. My aunts sat downstairs in a line, handing cups of tea and biscuits to my father, who was quite calm. He was always quite calm. My mother's sisters reacted in different ways to the noises coming from upstairs, the hurrying up and down of the midwife and the house servants.

'I remember when you were born, Dahlia,' Era said. 'You were so quick arriving, the doctors had hardly got here when there you were, crying.'

'But Pultoo – what an age he took!' Mary said. Pultoo, who was five, had been hustled away for the day with his father, taken to the law chambers to sit in a corner and play quietly with pen nibs and paper. He could always be distracted in this way: and it was thought it was not good for small boys to overhear the noises of childbirth. Whether because it would distress and frighten them, or because they would prove themselves nuisances, I do not know. But Pultoo reached his teenage years, as I did and my brother too, believing that babies were what happened after you were taken as a great treat to Nana's law chambers, playing all afternoon with stationery, inkwells and the junior clerks. With five married sisters and a sister-in-law by the time Pultoo was in his teenage years, the day-at-Papa's followed by a return home to find a new tight-swaddled and squashed-face niece-or-nephew became a regular, sometimes twice-annual event, like a festival.

'Pultoo surprised Mama, even,' Era said. 'She said she grew bored with waiting for him.'

'But it was so cold,' Nadira said. 'It was December, and we were all sitting over the fire in sweaters and coats, remember? Papa said he had never known it so cold. Pultoo was nice and warm, and he didn't want to come out.'

All her sisters hid their laughter behind their hands. 'Don't talk such nonsense,' Mary said, on account of my father. But my father paid no attention to anything his sisters-in-law said on any occasion, and he just passed his cup to Mary, who poured him another cup of tea.

'What are you going to do, Mahmood, after the baby is born?' Nadira said.

'Well, I shall be the baby's father, I suppose,' my father said. 'But that is not a full-time occupation. I expect I shall go on doing just what I have been doing, but with the addition of a small extra person.'

'What did you mean?' Mira asked Nadira.

'I meant whether he and Shiri and the dear little baby are going to stay in Dacca,' Nadira said. 'I so want to see the dear little baby every day.'

'You can see dear little baby Bubbly every day,' Mira said. 'And you never seem all that interested in her.'

'Oh, baby Bubbly,' Nadira said. 'Bubbly is getting old and fat and argumentative. One of these days, she is going to go to school, you mark my words. She's no fun at all.'

'Well, there's Sharmin's baby,' Mira said. 'We go to see pretty little Ejaj once a week. Won't he do?'

'Laddu's child,' Nadira said, superfluously. 'I don't count that the same at all.'

'Can I help you to anything, Mahmood?' Mary said.

'I would like some rosogollai, please,' my father said, and my aunt passed him the plate.

'Did Shiri ever succeed in finding a replacement cook, after you had to get rid of the old one?' Mary said. She set the plate down on the yellow teak table and, with a symmetrical gesture of her two forefingers, smoothed the two black wings of her hair behind her large, pointed, elfin ears.

'Well, she was obliged to take on a boy as a temporary replace- ment,' my father said, continuing very equably with social conver- sation while his younger sisters-in-law tried to settle his future. 'You see, when they heard that we were returning to Dacca for four months shortly—'

'But I just don't see,' Nadira said, 'why Shiri and Mahmood can't return to Dacca, now that they are going to have a baby.'

'Well, people don't stop having babies simply because they have to live in Barisal,' Era said. 'And that is where Mahmood's job is. He has to be there.'

'But I want them to come back,' Nadira said. 'I want to see the dear little baby every day. Mahmood, can't you leave Shiri here? I'm sure it's bad for her to travel with a baby.'

'Travel with a baby?' Era said, alarmed.

'What is that noise?' Mary said, and it was true: the quality of the noise from upstairs had changed. At the foot of the stairs, a woman stood, smiling: it was the midwife, and though she saw this every day, hundreds of times a year, she had not forgotten that this might be the most important day of the family's lives. And my father's composure now proved itself as thin as a wafer, because he rose with a look of transcendence and anxiety on his face. The midwife said that he had a son: she asked him to come upstairs to his wife and child.

'Is that the baby?' Nadira said. 'Has he really come? Am I an aunt now?'

6.

A week after my brother Zahid was born, my father went back to Barisal. My grandfather in person went down with him to the Dacca port at Sadarghat, where the tottering white four-storeyed launches to Barisal and other river towns departed. This was not a common thing to happen. My grandfather left his daughter and baby grandson at home and ceremonially escorted Mahmood to the port. There was something in his behaviour that expressed some retrospective dissatisfaction with his first grandson, Laddu's child. But my grandfather was always the sort of person who would enjoy the children of his daughters more. And Laddu had married a woman from West Pakistan in secret, even though the child was born when they had been admitted once more to the family. In time my grandfather would be reconciled to Laddu and Sharmin and their children, and would actually take their youngest son, Shibli, into his house to be raised entirely by himself and

148

Nani. But for the moment, Nana would not have walked Laddu to the end of the road to get a rickshaw. There was a grand and beneficent quality about his taking my father to the Barisal launch on this occasion. It was something to do with the new baby Zahid, sucking contentedly in the warmth of his grandfather's house in Rankin Street, turning his face with interest to the light falling through the mango leaves, or just idly basking with cross-faced assurance in the constant love, curiosity and excitement of his six aunts. The six aunts, particularly the smaller ones, were constantly waking him up from sleep to try to make him give them a smile and a kiss at this time of his life. They wanted him to confirm their belief that he was very dark and very clever, which Zahid did by blowing a bubble on his own and giving them a stern look at being woken up.

The aunts and my grandmother and mother assumed that Nana's surprising offer meant that he had something he needed to say to my father, perhaps shortly before saying goodbye to him. This was my grandfather's way on occasion: to give out a firm instruction to someone when he knew they would not have time to think anything over and respond to it. If this was so, no one knew what Nana said to Mahmood, in the cool high back of the Morris Oxford he drove at the time. I can see my father's face between the arches on the ferry's upper deck, thoughtful to the point of puzzlement; I can see Nana, the best-dressed man on the quay in his white shirt and charcoal-grey suit, giving a single confident wave upwards and turning back between earth-scented bales of jute and tea, walking through the noise of the crowd. There he goes; stepping among the squashed fruit of the market at the gates of the old pink waterfront palace, past the line of hole-in-the-wall barbers' shops, the paper-bag manufacturers with their antique scales, the small engine shops that so frightened me as a child with their glimpse into a world of black oil and obscured metal intricacies. He walks among noise and filth, ignoring the blandishments of the rickshaw-wallahs with the unimpeded step of someone who knows he has given clear and easy instructions.

Bubbly, mending socks, fetching clean jars of water for Pultoo
when he was at the easel painting, or even cleaning his brushes
for him – they were great admirers of Pultoo's early work. Their
limit came only with baby Shibli, whom they were prepared to
coo over but not to bear responsibility for. Most of all, they made
themselves useful by being pleasant and humble about the house,
never intruding or making noise. The room they shared made no
extra work for the servants. Nani might have disliked their
constant grinding of paan with a pestle, the two of them sitting
quietly in a corner muttering trivialities. They were keen observers,
from their window, of the comings and goings of the neighbourhood, and always wanted to know when they glimpsed a child
who he or she could possibly be. But, on the whole, nobody minded
them being there, and it was with some surprise that Pultoo
remarked one day that it must be a year since his two grand-
mothers had come to stay in Dhanmondi.

2.

The house of Khandekar, Nana's great friend, was quite different.
When the roadblocks allowed, and there were fewer soldiers on
the streets making a nuisance of themselves, Nana often went
round there for some civilized company. There were only two
sons, both students at the university, both clever, respectful, well-
read boys, who would be a credit to their parents and to the legal
profession. Khandekar and his wife had their home to themselves.
There were never great crowds of daughters, sons-in-law and
grandchildren demanding attention; never a party of cousins from
the village muttering among themselves and asking to help with
the preparation of food. Nobody threatened to dry mangoes on
Khandekar's balcony. It was pleasant to visit for an hour or two,
take a cup of tea; to continue the argument about a law suit, to
chat quietly about the state of affairs, to drift back under the

189

portico, with the rich, jam-like scent of mimosa and jasmine, to the pleasant subject of their student days in Calcutta. It was good to laugh and banter and forget the world altogether, as much as they could.

Nana would have gone to Khandekar's house every day if he could. But all too often, however, it proved impossible to get from one house to another, even though they were separated by only a ten-minute journey. Roadblocks sprang up overnight; bands of soldiers loitered at corners; men who in other times would have been the refuse of the street appeared out of nowhere, demanding papers with threats and refusing to state the source of their authority. There were many such people, these days, and they were especially evident about Khandekar's house. Many of them were Bihari, who had never felt at home, had always been dissatisfied among the Bengalis. It was impossible to know in advance whether one would get to the end of one's journey unmolested. My grandfather was not accustomed to put up with the impudence of soldiers and badmashes demanding papers. But he saw that there was no point in fighting it. He gloomily observed over the dinner table that, like an old-fashioned Munshi, he would soon have to forbid the women of his family to leave the house. The women of his family objected. But he laid down the law, and none of them, not even Nani, was ever allowed to go on a visit, or to the market, without taking Rustum to sit by them and stare down the soldiery. To Khandekar's house, they could not go at all, not unless they went with him. Just by there the roadblocks shifted, repositioned, multiplied. Across the road, from side to side, mysterious and unproductive workmen spread, making the way impassable. Once, a huge demonstration appeared from nowhere, blocking the roads in that quarter for hours. It turned out to be a demonstration of loyalty to the government in West Pakistan, and therefore hired for this specific occasion. Sometimes it was possible to reach Khandekar's house, so very few streets away, by ingenious means. But often those ingenious means failed; no resourceful improvisation on Rustum's part could circumvent protesters, roadblocks, security checks, puffed-up and paid-for Biharis, or ersatz roadworks. The authorities were bending all their ingenuity on blocking these streets, because a few houses away from Khandekar lived Sheikh Mujib.

These days, Sheikh Mujib's face was everywhere in Dacca. His candidacy to become prime minister had spread and spread, and his face was on every wall. His thick glasses, his open, trustworthy, intelligent face promised that things would change. He was no longer seen at Sufiya's, and his usual enjoyment of walking in the street had come to an end. Occasionally there was a genuine demonstration outside Sheikh Mujib's house in support of him. Several times, Sheikh Mujib had made an appearance before bigger crowds, calling for some measure of independence. It was two years since the government had clamped down on statements of Bengal nationhood – meaning poetry, music, images. What would happen, people started to ask, if a Bengali were elected president of the whole country – if the capital of Pakistan were moved to Dacca, the first language of the nation became Bengali, and the national anthem became a song of Tagore's? It was unthinkable. But there was no obvious reason why it should not happen – Nana and Khandekar agreed on this. There were more voters in East Pakistan than in West Pakistan, and they were less divided. There might be no democratic reason why Sheikh Mujib should not be elected president of the divided country, and make his first presidential speech in the language of Dacca, to an immense crowd of Bengalis, on the banks of the Padma. Was there any reason why not? What would happen if it came to pass? The authorities did not propose to find out. Hence the fake roadworks and the hired demonstrators and the security checks, blocking in Sheikh Mujib's house. They often prevented visitors to his near neighbours, too, such as Khandekar, to my grandfather's immense irritation, as I said.

'I am astonished you reached us,' Khandekar said, coming to the door himself as my grandfather came in. 'Astonished. We were waiting yesterday all day for my wife's brother to visit, and the day before that, and the day before that, but nothing. He was turned back three, four times. What is your secret, my dear fellow?'

'I have no idea,' Nana said. 'I have not the foggiest idea. This is a very strange situation. Some days you cannot leave your house before being harassed; others you sail through without the smallest disturbance. I did see that the goons were drawn up the road somewhat, besieging your distinguished neighbour. Rustum said, "If I drive this way and that way, and double back, and then through and across and in between – then we shall reach our destination without the smallest trouble." And so it proved.'

'Ah, Rustum, resourceful fellow,' Khandekar said. 'Ask him to take his tea in the kitchen – we are lucky to have such people by us. My wife is joining us.'

My grandfather greeted Mrs Khandekar, neat and shining, something like excitement in her face.

'I was just saying,' Khandekar said to her, in a loud voice, 'how lucky it is to have a driver like Rustum, a clever, resourceful fellow like that. We will have tea in the study today. There. The truth is –' Mr Khandekar said, in a lower voice, having shut the door to his study and invited my grandfather to sit on the beige sofa underneath the bookcase '– the truth is that last week, my wife and I were talking on the upper veranda, quite innocuously, when I observed, over the wall, a pair of official goons standing in the street. They were evidently listening to what we were saying. Here, we will not be listened to.'

'If it were just the goons in the street!' Mrs Khandekar burst out. 'But when the listeners are within one's own house . . .'

'Surely—'

'I am afraid so,' Khandekar said. 'We strongly suspect that one or more of the servants are listening to our conversations. We could hardly believe it at first.'

'They have been with us for decades,' Mrs Khandekar said, 'every one of them. But I see that money and threats are greater things than loyalty in this world.'

192

'We cannot trust anyone,' Khandekar said. 'Do not trust anyone, my dear friend – not Rustum, not the gardener. Perhaps especially not Laddu's wife.'

'Oh, surely not Sharmin,' my grandfather said. 'She is quite one of the family now. I cannot believe—'

'Perhaps she is to be trusted,' Khandekar said. 'But what about her family? Are you sure that no cousin of hers, no uncle in Lahore ever asks her friendly questions about her husband's family? How could she not answer such questions, and how could she know what use the answers would be put to?'

'My dear Khandekar,' my grandfather said, 'if there were anything whatsoever that would interest the authorities in my family's—' He stopped. Evidently he thought at this moment about his beautiful library, concealed behind a plaster wall in the cellar. He had heard his daughters speak about it as a great joke among themselves. It had never occurred to him that Sharmin should be excluded from such conversations, and it would never have occurred to his daughters. But how simple for a cousin or uncle of Sharmin to ask a question or two, to discover so interesting and comment-worthy a fact! 'My dear Khandekar,' he began again, in a lower voice, 'surely you don't have anything to conceal. You lead so blameless a life. No authority could concoct a case against you on any grounds. It would be making bricks without straw.'

Khandekar and his wife exchanged looks. They were unreadable looks. My grandfather, horrified, came to an easy conclusion. His oldest friend was consulting his wife to discover whether he could be trusted. For a moment, he thought of getting up and leaving. But then he observed to himself that the situation would pass. The suspicion shadowing Khandekar's mind was unworthy, but perhaps nothing could be ruled out, with the soldiery rampaging through the street, unchecked. What pressures had been brought to bear, and what obligations called in – one never knew that about the oldest of old friends. So my grandfather forgave Khandekar, and Khandekar never knew that he had been forgiven for anything in particular.

And then the look between Khandekar and his wife proved a responsible one, because Khandekar's wife gave a small, tight, satisfied smile. 'The boys,' Khandekar said in a low voice. 'They have gone. No one knows. The servants all believe that they have gone to stay with their uncle, my wife's brother the civil engineer, in Chittagong.'

'But they have not,' my grandfather said.

'No,' Mrs Khandekar said. 'No, they have not.'

The tea was brought, and for some moments they talked of trivialities. There were few trivialities to be had in those days. Future plans, current activities, social life, mutual friends – all seemed to be tinged with disaster. We Bengalis, we love to talk, on any subject and on none, but the men in the street, the stench of their breath had entered Khandekar's study, and silence fell, unaccountably, between the three of them. The boy who brought the tea was familiar to my grandfather, his face politely lowered behind the tea tray. He had been with Khandekar's family for ten years, at the very least. How could such a man be suspected of anything, of deserving silence?

At length, the boy withdrew, leaving the tea things. Mrs Khandekar poured it out herself, as she liked to. After a decent pause, listening to the boy's noisy retreat in the hallway, she said, 'The boys have gone, you see.'

'Next week,' Khandekar said, 'Mujib will win this election. No one can doubt it. He will win it fair and square.'

'There is no doubt about that,' my grandfather said.

'And then what happens?' Khandekar said, his voice lowered. 'Of course, it is clear what will not happen. Mujib will not become Prime Minister of this country. He will not be invited to take up his position. How could that happen? Those people over there, they have gone to the effort of suppressing songs – *songs*, my dear old friend. What efforts do you suppose they will go to to suppress the result of something important, like an election, to make sure that the result is to their taste?'

'I have seen the soldiers outside,' my grandfather said. 'I know what you say is right.'

'The boys have gone,' Mrs Khandekar said again. 'It is best if they leave now, not after the election. We do not know what will happen once the election takes place. They have gone somewhere in readiness for any eventuality. I do not know where. It was best not to know.'

My grandfather nodded. He understood. They were good, brave boys, the Khandekar sons. One of them would be killed in due course, fighting against the Pakistanis for the independence of Bangla Desh. Vulgar people afterwards tried to describe that son as a martyr, but in later years, Khandekar and Mrs Khandekar would have no truck with such comments. They kept his photograph on the sideboard in their house, the one that I came to be familiar with when I made a visit with my grandfather in later years. The other, the younger of the two, returned after the war and continued with his studies, becoming, in the end, a very senior public administrator whom I always found cold and frightening to deal with. But all that lay far in the future. For the moment, the two boys had gone, and were preparing to fight for the freedom of their country in the struggle to come, though the expression 'freedom-fighter' was not yet coined. Where they were, the Khandekars did not know, or were not saying.

'If I may give my old friend some firm advice,' Khandekar said.

My grandfather nodded.

'Have your family around you. Ask them to come and stay in your house. Nobody knows how bad things may get. You will want to have them around you, to know that they are safe.'

At that moment, outside, as if to confirm Khandekar's advice, there was a shriek of brakes and a short burst of gunfire. There had been gunfire in the streets before, but remote, and possible to mistake for fireworks. This was close. There was no possibility of thinking that it was anything else. 'Rustum!' my grandfather called. 'Rustum!'

It was difficult to express what my grandfather might have been fearing, but he got up and opened the door into the hallway, and Rustum was emerging from the kitchen, wiping his mouth, with a puzzled expression. Behind him was a tall, thin man with neatly combed hair and a very clean white shirt.

'We are nearly finished in here,' said Mrs Khandekar, to this second man. 'Thank you for your patience.'

My grandfather did not know it – he did not recognize this man, though he had been in the same room as him a dozen times and he must have been faintly familiar. He did not recognize him, even though he was carrying his well-polished harmonium. It was Altaf, visiting at the suggestion of Mrs Khandekar, who had a particular task she wanted him to carry out.

3.

Nana wasted no time. As soon as he got home, again succeeding in avoiding the roadblocks, he went upstairs to his office and wrote three well-argued letters. He sealed them, addressed them, and sent Rustum out to deliver them to Laddu; to Mahmood and Shiri; and to Era, newly married and living twenty minutes' drive away. Rustum told them that Advocate-sahib had told him to wait for a response, so he sat in the kitchen of each house, and waited for the discussion to finish, and a reply to be written. Finally, he returned home. It was very late at night by the time his task was done. And it was a good day that my grandfather chose to send these messages round by hand. It would not be long before a curfew was imposed by the military authorities, and Rustum, driving about Dacca after dark, would have been shot on sight.

In my grandfather's house, there were already living Nana and Nani, of course. The unmarried daughters were there, Mary, Mira, Nadira, Dahlia, and ten-year-old Bubbly, in that house without books, without the harmonium, where the possessions were spaced out in ways that had grown familiar in the last year or so. Pultoo was also still there, a thoughtful, quiet boy, good at occupying himself, and Boro-mama's son Shibli, who was a sturdy child, walking and talking now. There were also the two great-grandmothers, Nana's two mothers, and some cousins who had come in the last month from the village, and were remaining there. Now the other children, the ones married and away from home, read Nana's letters. They all decided that they must follow his instructions, and come back home for the sake of safety.

Era and her new husband were the first to arrive, the very next morning; they came with suitcases, as if for a very few days. And then Boro-mama and Sharmin came the next day with their other three children, wan and puzzled. Their possessions were innumerable and small, and several journeys back and forth were needed before all of them were piled up in the hallway of Grandfather's house. 'Look, it's Daddy,' Dahlia said to Shibli, but he clung to her legs. For him, his mother and father were glamorous visitors, seen at weekends, and though he would play with his brothers and sister when asked to, he always gave the impression of playing alongside them, rather than with, always happier to retreat into his world of wooden blocks, singing a small song to himself. His father came to him and lifted him up into the air, making a puffing noise. Boro-mama's sisters could have told him that, of all things, Shibli hated being lifted from the ground. His cries filled the house, and eventually, when his father set him back down again and let him run back to his aunt Dahlia, they coagulated into words. 'Do not do that!' he cried. 'Do not do that! I am absolutely frightened when you do that to me!'

'Oh dear,' Nani said.

But in an hour Shibli, comforted with a sweet, was sitting quite contentedly by the side of his sister – his brothers, five and seven years older than him, considered themselves men like their father, and Shibli was unmistakably a child happiest when surrounded and pampered by ladies. His sister, resigned to her task, was nearer his age, and imbued with the duty of being a good little girl – her aunts privately thought her dull. She had recently learnt to read, and was turning the pages of her picture book for Shibli's benefit. His eyes, however, went round the crowded room.

'I don't see how we are to manage,' Boro-mama said.

'It is better that you are here,' Nani said briskly. These arrangements would not be for so very long, she assured him, wondering whether this was, in fact, the case. She looked about the room. Not everyone staying, or living in the house was there. Some of the girls were in their rooms, occupying themselves in privacy. But even so, it seemed very crowded already. Outside, in the street, there was a shout, followed by another shout, further away. Men's voices in this quiet street were not that common. It could not be understood what the voices had called. But the tone of command and acknowledgement was unmistakable; the tone of military command. Nana, retreating from the sitting room to go and sit in quiet upstairs, paused and gave a questioning look to Nani.

'Are the gates shut and bolted?' she said, to nobody in particular.

'Bolted?' said one of the great-grandmothers – they were both sitting on the two-seater sofa, upright and occupied with darning. 'Bolted?'

'What did she say?' the other great-grandmother said, the bigger, more assertive one. 'Bolted? What for? It's the middle of the afternoon.'

'Rustum shut the gates,' Boro-mama said. 'I don't know if he bolted them.'

'He bolted them,' Era said. 'Did he bolt them?'

'And Shiri has not yet come,' Nana said. 'She must not arrive to find herself bolted out.'

'Those were soldiers,' Mary said, in a low voice to Era. 'Those were soldiers, in the street. They were right outside the gate, just in the street, just there.'

'I wish Shiri would come,' Era said. 'And then we could bolt the gates and feel safe.'

4.

Sheikh Mujib won the election. For the first time since the founding of the two-part country, the leader of the country would represent the eastern half. But nothing happened; he was arrested; he was released; and then he made a speech announcing the independence of the Bengalis, and was arrested again. For many days, the sounds from the streets were of student protests, of shouting and chanting and the noise of official warnings, made over the loudspeakers. Finally, the Pakistanis came over, and began to have discussions with Mujib about his demands. But nobody believed in any of these discussions, and the protests continued and grew. People said – Khandekar, for instance, told my grandfather – that the commercial flights from West Pakistan to Dacca were full these days. Full of young, fit men with short hair, moving with purpose. Many people believed that these men were Pakistani soldiers in mufti, coming in large numbers to prepare for a crackdown.

My father, in the sitting room in Elephant Road, read his father-in-law's letter, requesting that they up sticks and go to stay with him for the time being, and his brow furrowed.

'How many are they, living there?' he asked my mother. She did not know.

'A lot,' he said. 'We are better off here.' It was true that the six of us had our own space, there in Elephant Road. The house was as secure as my grandfather's, which was only a short distance away, and even if the storm broke, they could stay where they were, communicating with my mother's family by telephone. So, for the moment, my mother and father decided that we would not move, and my mother tried to calm Nana down in a telephone call. My brother had his own room; my sisters shared a room; and the baby slept at the foot of my parents' bed. That baby was me: I had been born only a very few months before, and everybody called me Saadi. In any case, my father went on to say, there

199

was the family downstairs, who were well connected and would see to our safety, whatever happened.

The next morning they awoke to the sound of an air-raid siren. In front of the house, there were two tanks of the Pakistani Army, pointing the barrels of their guns over the wall and directly at the front bedrooms of the house.

My mother hurried downstairs to try to understand what had happened. There, she learnt that the brother of their landlord, who had been serving in the Pakistani Air Force in a very senior capacity, had deserted on hearing that Sheikh Mujib had been arrested and the results of the election declared null and void. Where he was, nobody knew. He was what my father referred to when he said that the family downstairs had very good connections. It had turned out that they had very bad connections, or so it seemed, in those days. The military authorities had decided that the house in Elephant Road bore some sort of responsibility for the desertion, and the guns were pointed directly at them and, of course, at us.

My mother screamed and fainted and revived herself. She accused my father of leaving them in terrible danger, when they could have left the day before, or the day before that; they could have been secure in her father's house, where nobody could seriously discover a danger or a threat. Nobody would point a tank at her father's house; nobody in their family was in a position to desert. In a spirit of pure terror, she picked up the telephone and tried to dial. But that was too late, also. There was no dialling tone. Looking out of the window, she saw that the telephone wires to the house had been cut. They hung like a mop from the telegraph pole.

There was no means of getting out of the house, and soon a van with a loudspeaker went by, announcing a general curfew with immediate effect. That had been what the air-raid siren had warned of. When my parents listened to the radio, they discovered the detail of the general curfew called by the Pakistani Army. Not everyone was prevented from leaving their houses by the presence of a tank against the front wall. But everyone in Dacca was barred inside, on pain of death. It was 25 March. As that long day went on, the children bored and fractious and not understanding, the vengeance of the army on the rest of Dacca intruded on the street. Somewhere in the middle distance, a great plume of smoke was rising. Something was burning, or being burnt: something substantial, and rather nearer, from time to time, screams and shouts and the rattle of gunfire; very near, the metallic, clipped announcements through loud-hailers, announcing the penalty of death.

The radio had nothing to say about any of that. It was only much later that people learnt the army had gone into the poor parts of Dacca and burnt them to the ground; that the university had been entered and set to the torch. Afterwards, the dead came to be reckoned, but at the time, there was only black smoke and, too near, fire and shots. My mother and father, my brothers and sisters and I went to the back room of the house and passed the time as best we could. From time to time the neighbours downstairs came up to see how we were. But they knew no more than anyone else, and they could not comfort or explain the situation.

'They are going to blow up the house,' my mother said, and, without meaning to, she started screaming. 'If only we had gone to Papa's – they are going to break in and kill us, they will, they will kill us all.'

'We have done nothing wrong,' my father said.

'They are going to kill us,' my mother said. 'They will.' My brother, eleven years old, understood, and looked at her with solemn, frightened eyes. He was not familiar with the display of fear by the adults of his family. Quietly, I slept on.

The next day, the cook came into the salon early. 'There are people on the streets,' he said. It was around eight thirty. 'On bicycles and in cars, moving around normally.' The radio, when switched on, announced that the curfew would be lifted for a short time that day to allow people to fetch supplies and food. It would be reimposed, however, at one, and anyone found wandering the streets would be shot on sight. My father went into the front room of the house. Even after a day, it had the musty, miserable air of an uncared-for house returned to after a long holiday. Cautiously, he went to the windows. The street was empty; there was no one moving. More remarkably, the two tanks were gone. He tried not to look at what he saw at the end of the road, lying in the dirt.

'Where are you going?' my mother said, coming out of the back room with the baby in her arms. My father was going downstairs. 'We have to get to Father's house. We cannot stay here. They are going to kill us.'

'No, you and the children mustn't stay,' my father said, carrying on his way downstairs, quite calmly. 'You must go while you can.'

'But how?' my mother said. 'How are we to get a message to them? There is no telephone.'

From downstairs, my father's voice drifted up. 'You must pack a bag for you and the children,' he called. 'Do it quickly. Only what you need.'

Nothing seemed clear to my mother, but she did what she was told. She quietened the children, pretending as best she could that this was all some great adventure, and told Zahid that he must make sure the others made no noise, and stayed exactly where they were, in the back rooms of the house. Her main terror was that a child of hers, standing at the front window of the upper storey, would be seen by a passing soldier and shot for no reason. And then a miracle happened: a familiar engine noise in the street outside. She hesitatingly went herself to the front window. There, below, in the street, was the red Vauxhall car. Rustum, my grandfather's driver, got out hurriedly, looking quickly to left and right. He left the car's engine running, and the driver's door open. He banged on the gate of the house, but my mother was already taking her half-packed bags, one in each hand, and calling for the children. Behind her, Zahid and the girls were following, their faces pale. 'Where is Saadi?' my mother said. I had been left sleeping peacefully in the back bedroom. 'Go, go, go,' she said to Sushmita. 'Go and pick up your little brother. Do you think you can carry him?' Sushmita thought she could, and the five of us went swiftly downstairs. From the other flat, my father emerged and, sweeping us along, brought up the rear. My mother dropped the suitcase on the ground, and fumblingly opened the bolt of the front gate. 'I never said goodbye,' she said to my father, meaning to the neighbours downstairs.

'Go on, go on,' my father said impatiently, and between them, he and Rustum bundled my mother and the four children into the back of the red Vauxhall. Quite suddenly, the back door of the car was shut; Rustum got into the driver's seat. 'You go on,' my father said. 'I shall come along later today.' From the outside, he banged on the roof to tell Rustum to go.

'What is it? What are you doing?' my mother mouthed from the back of the car, but it was too late. My father had turned and gone back inside the house in Elephant Road, shutting and bolting the gate behind him, and again my mother, secure in the back of the red Vauxhall, began to scream. This time I awoke and, responding to my mother's screams, began to wail myself. She had had no idea my father would not come with us until he had shut the door of the car and banged a practical, necessary farewell on the roof.

It had been only fifteen minutes since the lifting of the curfew for five hours was announced on the radio. At one o'clock it would fall again. Nana must have ordered Rustum to go straight out and fetch us.

5.

Elephant Road was only a ten-minute drive from my grandfather's house. It was quite a different sort of place. There were small shops, selling groceries and household necessities; it was, in normal times, a pleasant, busy thoroughfare. There was a large Bata store, which acted as a landmark in Dacca, and other shoe shops, carpet sellers, hardware emporia, with rows of plastic bowls and aluminium pans hanging outside, tea stalls, confectioners, copper show-pieces, barbers, chemists and sherwani-merchants.

I slept peacefully through the short journey from Elephant Road to Nana's house in Dhanmondi. My mother, brother and sisters would never forget what they saw. The windows of Sushmita's favourite confectioner, the one with the best jelapi, the one where she loved to hang around and watch the expert confectioner piping a map of the world, a round Arabic signature, a piece of magical writing in the seething oil and let it rise; the windows of that shop were smashed. Inside, there was broken glass and spattered confectionery, milk and flour and sugar thrown like abstract fantasies across the oil-soaked floor. A house was on fire, its gates hanging from their hinges. The hardware shops had given up their contents, like great vomiting beasts. Across the street, pans and tools and plastic goods were strewn and crushed. And there was a rickshaw, turned over, lying in the street abandoned. 'There's blood on it – there's blood on it!' Sushmita screamed. There was; and underneath it was lying some kind of large packet, slumped and crushed.

'Don't look,' Rustum said. 'We'll soon be nice and safe.' But they had to look. Down a side-street, there was a platoon of the military, lounging against the cab of a lorry and paying no attention to the shop further down that was on fire, the gusts of flame and black smoke pouring into the street like great foul-fragrant blooms. It must have been one of the shops that made a good living renting out splendid garments in silver and thread-of-gold to guests at weddings; all that glitter and light, consumed in a moment. And one of the shop's mannequins – no, more than one had been dragged out of the shop and thrown into the road, lying there in an awkward position. Perhaps the person who had done it had wanted to steal the outfits from the mannequins, because they were quite bare, the arms raised, waxlike in the mud of the street, and more blood covering one mannequin's chest and running into a black stain on the road. But it was no mannequin. 'Don't look,' Rustum said again. Sushmita would never forget that sight: a man lying in the road, his throat cut, his fat little legs raised as if in an attempt to run. And then she was sick.

'Please, Rustum,' my mother said, when they were drawing up outside Nana's house. 'Please, just leave us here and go back for my husband.'

'It is too dangerous,' Rustum said. 'He would not come. He will come later. I can't go and make him get in the car. If he didn't come, it's because he has important things that he has to do.'

'He has to come,' my mother said, but now Rustum was out of the car and opening the gate. There were no soldiers to be seen. 'If you won't go, I shall go myself.'

Rustum ignored this, and between him, Nana, Nani and Boro-mama, who had all come out of the house, my mother and all of us were bundled together into safety. The children, Shiri and the baby came through the glass-framed porch at the side of the house, and were propelled by the servants and others along the passageway and into the large salon at the back of the house. My mother was screaming in terror, screaming for her husband, and Rustum explained how it was that my father had been left behind. Nana's face seemed to age in a moment. 'Have mercy,' my grandmother said, and led my mother away.

My sisters were handed over to Shibli's ayah who took them upstairs to clean them up and make them respectable again. My brother Zahid, who had observed everything in silence, went over to his aunts, who greeted him politely, as if he were a grown-up and paying a visit. In twenty minutes, the noises of grief from Nani's room had subsided a little; and Zahid had found an interesting book to occupy himself with in a corner. For the moment, I was sleeping peacefully, swaddled in my blanket, guarded by Dahlia-aunty. The gates were shut and bolted. Outside, in the Dhanmondi street, the noises of battle, the crackle that a house on fire makes began to return.

205

6.

Many people had taken the same decision that my family had, and gone to wherever they could be together. They felt that they could best sit out the curfew if they knew where everyone was, and could feel reassured. One of these families was in a house only two streets away from my grandfather's. It was also a white courtyard house, very much in the same Bauhaus style, and there was, too, a large coconut palm at the front and a pair of green-painted gates against the street. In this house, which belonged to an important businessman, were living their children, two sons and two daughters, the eldest thirty-three, the youngest only nineteen. The two eldest were sons, and married, and their young wives were with them. There were also two grandchildren: a boy of four and a baby, which had been born only weeks before, to the younger son's wife. All these people had moved to the same house by the first day of the curfew, the day that we had been in Elephant Road with the guns of the tanks pointing directly at us.

All that day, the soldiery had roamed the street. They had not hesitated to shoot at anyone, even rickshaw drivers, who had been seen out, breaking the law. When they saw a shop with a Hindu proprietor, or one where they knew a grudge could be borne, they broke in. They threw the stock, whether sweets, or meat, or cloth, or paper, or books, or shirts, into the road. They poured petrol on to whatever they could find and set a match to it. Then they sat back and watched it burn. They drove to the university, and set fire to one of the main buildings. 'Intellectuals,' the soldiers said to each other. Another troop drove into the shanty town, where the buildings were made of wood and hardboard. There was no curfew observance here: the inhabitants lived half outside, and had no gates to close. The settlement burnt at the touch of a match.

The soldiery had been given orders, but there were just too

many of them. They kept meeting up with the same patrols, bellowing curfew orders into loudspeakers. And at some point, one tank patrol found its way into Dhanmondi, and outside the house with the green gates.

Afterwards, my family always believed that these soldiers had not found their way by chance to this house. We believed that there were families living in Dhanmondi who believed in the unity of the state; who did not speak Bengali much, and thought of those who did as traitors. Some of those families were happy to tell the roaming soldiery the houses from which rebel songs could be heard; where the flag of an independent Bangla Home had been raised from the roof. Perhaps, too, houses where they might find traitors who could easily be punished in an immediate way; even young women.

Some of these families who gave out such information, who directed the forces to particular houses during the war, went on living where they did after the war. Everyone knew who they were. They kept to themselves, and in after years, we children were not permitted to play with the children of such families.

In any case, perhaps the soldiers found their way to this house by chance. Perhaps they just heard something within, without paying for advice. A sound was coming from the house, a thin, high crying. It was a hungry baby. The soldiers knew that where there was a baby crying, there were young women. This was a rich area, but that meant nothing any more. The patrol hammered on the green gates of the house, and, when no response came, they got in their tank and drove directly at it. The white walls of the house fell inwards, into the garden.

'What is it?' the businessman was shouting, as he came out of his house – even then, he continued believing that he was living in the world he knew from a week ago. He did not see how things had changed, or he would not have come out shouting in outrage. The commander pushed him aside and went into the house. Five women – four young, one middle-aged, one nursing the baby that had been making the noise – were in what seemed to be the salon.

They stood up as eight of the soldiers stamped into the house; the mother made a gesture as if to draw her daughters to her. But one daughter – a plump-faced, pretty girl in a silver-edged sari – broke away and ran out of the french windows into the garden. Where was she thinking of going? There was no escape there. And if there had been an escape, that would have been breaking the curfew, and they could have shot her. Three soldiers followed her out, easily overtaking her and throwing her down on the ground. There was no difficulty in holding her shoulders to the earth while another soldier forced her legs apart, raising her sari. A fist went over her mouth, and a terrible stifled yell was all the protest she could make.

In the house, there was a single shot. The women screamed, and went on screaming. In a few moments, the soldiers killed the other brother, too, with two shots, then a third, and then the father, in the same way. But they did not kill the women until they had raped all of them. One of them, as she was borne down by the terrible weight of the men, tried to grasp and steal the pistol in the captain's holster. But her arms were held down, and she could not reach. The captain took out the pistol and waved it in her face, before hitting her hard on one side, then on the other, then again; there was the sound and the strange sensation, like wooden bricks moving about in a soft bag, of her jaw breaking under the blow. Then they raped her again.

They did not waste a bullet on the baby, but killed it with a knife they took from the kitchen. The howling child went the same way. Under the table, two manservants cowered, their hands over their heads, shaking, backwards and forwards, clutching at each other. What were the soldiery going to do with them? Nothing. They could spread the word. That was what would happen.

For ever afterwards, my family wondered how it was that Nana knew what the soldiers had done, and what they were capable of. From the start of the curfew, he was determined that not only should nobody step outside the house but that the house should seem to be empty. Nadira-aunty believed and said that there was no need for such precautions. She did not believe that the Pakistani Army would enter any house if there was no threat and the inhabitants were obeying the curfew faithfully.

'That is how it is to be,' Nana said quietly. 'Nobody is to make any noise, or light a lamp. This house is to seem empty, without interest, vacated. You are not to draw attention to this house. When night falls, we sit in the dark or we go to bed.'

My grandfather would not share what he knew about what had happened in the businessman's house, two streets away. There were many such stories in Dacca that day, and for weeks into the future. The rapes and murders of the businessman's family was the one my grandfather knew about. The two man-servants whom the soldiery had left cowering under the kitchen table had waited there, expecting their deaths, until the point where the platoon had driven away. They had emerged from their inadequate hiding place, slowly taking their hands off their heads. The curfew was still in force, and if they left the house and walked on the street, they would be shot. There was, however, a back way through the gardens of the houses that could take them to somewhere safe. They were, as it happens, friends or perhaps even relations of Rustum, my grandfather's chauffeur, and they thought of going to him. They knew my grandfather was a powerful man; they might have known that he had had some dealings with the authorities, and they might have believed that he and his household were in some way protected from the worst of the events. They decided to make their way to my grandfather's house. It would mean crossing two streets, out in the open. But only two. They could risk that. And there was no question of remaining in this house. The worst of the events lay, defiled, in the sitting room and the garden. There was only one way they could take, and they were obliged to start by going into the garden next door. For the two man-servants, passing through those scenes was the worst thing either of them ever had to do.

7.

When my father had waved goodbye to his wife and children, he went back inside the house. The neighbours downstairs were waiting for him. He had discussed the situation with them, and had agreed that he could help them to leave the city as quickly as possible. So when he went inside their house, he found them sitting in their chairs with fraught expressions, three suitcases in front of them. They had not managed to pack very much.

The wife was crying, quite helplessly, and the children – two young men, thirteen and sixteen years old – were trying to comfort her. My father had already established, in conversations with their father, that nobody knew what had happened to their uncle, the distinguished air-force officer who had abruptly deserted three days before. It was clear that they would have to leave the house as quickly as possible. The house was being watched, and there was no possibility of them leaving on foot with suitcases without being arrested immediately. My father had agreed to help them to safety, before going to his father-in-law's house in Dhanmondi.

My father left the house, walking two hundred yards to the busy intersection where the cycle-rickshaws normally sat. He tried not to see what was to the left and to the right of him. Despite everything, there were two cycle-rickshaws sitting at their normal place, and he summoned both of them. Ignoring the four men on the opposite side of the road, hunched up and observant, he went back into the house. The younger child and the mother, veiling her face, came out and got into one rickshaw, which drove off northwards, towards Gulistan. Twenty minutes later, the father, alone, came out and took the second rickshaw in the opposite direction. Neither party had any luggage, and they were informally dressed. It was important to give the impression that they had gone out only for half an hour or an hour, perhaps to buy food, perhaps to ensure the safety of others. The second boy and my father stayed behind; the watchers would know something was happening if all the family left the house at the same time.

In an hour, an unfamiliar car drew up outside, and my father, in the most casual way imaginable, came out to hail the driver. With the telephone wires cut, how had my father got a message to his old college friend, living half a mile away? Nobody knew – it must have been a note, delivered by a servant of ours or of the family downstairs. The watchers opposite did not move, even when my father came out with three suitcases, one, two, three, helped by the gardener's boy in a grubby shirt and gloves, and loaded them into the boot of the car. My father was not their concern. They did not register when the gardener's boy, having loaded the three suitcases into the boot and shut the door on my father's side, went back to the gate of the house and shut it from the street side. The boy stepped into the car in the most natural way possible, and it drove off. It was only much later in the day, when the army officers came to discover what had been happening to the house of the traitor's brother, that they reflected that the gardener in the house was, after all, a much older man who had not been seen for some time, and he had never had a boy to help him out at all. But by that time the family who lived downstairs had disappeared, and could not be traced.

Their destination was a house in the quieter north of Dacca, away from the fighting and protests and the bodies in the streets, in Mohakhali. The three parties – the mother and younger son, the father, both in rickshaws, and my father and the elder son, looking like the gardener's boy, in a car with the family's luggage – reached the house in Mohakhali by different routes, some quite complicated. Everywhere, the streets were filled with rickshaws heavily laden with luggage; at the sides of the road, families were trying to hail private cars, begging to be taken away. In the course of their journey, my father heard about what had been done in the previous twenty-four hours – the monuments desecrated, the university buildings destroyed, the people shot. Anyone who had raised a flag of the Bengali Home above their house had been targeted. About him, sitting incongruously in the back of the car with a dirty and shivering teenage boy, my father could see the abandoned and charred results of a day of violence.

My father's first idea had been to go, in pretence, to my grandfather's house in Dhanmondi, as if the suitcases really were his. But he saw how impossible that would be. He could trick my mother once, but not twice, and she would not let him go. So the car drove in a large circuit through Dacca, stopping once or twice as if on urgent errands. My father's resourcefulness ran out: he found himself going into paper-merchants and butchers and a hardware store when he saw a rare one that was not looted or destroyed, and had opened today. The mother's journey was similar: she left the cycle-rickshaw where it was, and went into shops and immediately out again; once she made a pretence of paying off the cycle-rickshaw and went into a large shoe emporium; the rickshaw cycled off, but in reality made a large circle through the streets and picked her and her son up at the shop's other entrance, seven minutes later. From there, she made her way to the safe-house in Mohakhali. There were other tricks and dodges, though none of them knew if they were really being followed, many entrances into houses and shops and swift exits at other points, much bold innocent play-acting among the wreckage and bodies of Dacca on the morning of 26 March 1971.

By twelve o'clock, the family from downstairs in Elephant Road were safe for the moment in their friend's house in Mohakhali. My father had an hour to reach Dhanmondi, in a city where everyone was trying to flee in different directions for safety. After that, the curfew would begin and, promptly, the shooting.

8.

In my grandfather's house, there had been some trouble in finding space for everyone. Most of the household had gathered and discussed, and proposed different arrangements. The servants had almost all been sent out to buy as much food as they possibly could. The curfew had been lifted for a few hours today, but might be reimposed for the whole day tomorrow; and shortly there might be no food left in the shops. The servants were despatched to different markets and shopping streets in different parts of Dacca to buy food to see the large household through a week or two.

In making practical arrangements such as these, my mother, Shiri, generally took the lead. She was a well-organized and sensible person, who could be relied upon to give her sisters and the servants a task each that would contribute to a smooth-running machine. Her sisters were accustomed to ask her what they should do next and, despite his bluster and complaint, so was her elder brother Laddu. But today they were obliged to make the arrangements themselves, under the impatient direction of my grandmother. My mother had come into the house and collapsed on a sofa in the corner of the room, drawing her shawl about her head. There was nothing else she could do.

In her lap was a baby wrapped in blankets. For the moment I was sleeping. There were plenty of children in the house now – Boro-mama's children, my brother and sisters, and at least one aunt's children, too. I was the youngest, and the only one who had no understanding at all of what was happening. The other children, even the quite young ones, were old enough to understand that they must be quiet, and stay in their room without making any disturbance. Mary-aunty was supervising them, from the eleven-year-olds, like my brother Zahid, down to the little but sensible ones, like my sister Sunchita. They were playing some very quiet game, like Dead Crocodiles, in which the player who can stay absolutely still for the longest time wins the game; or perhaps Mary-aunty was reading all the children a long, quiet fairy story. Downstairs, my mother sobbed into her shawl as quietly as she knew how.

There was no word from my father. He had disappeared back

inside the house in Elephant Road without any explanation, without even waving goodbye. Nobody could understand it. He had to be following shortly – there was nothing to keep him in the house, and he must understand how dangerous it would be to remain in the same place as the family of a deserting senior officer. His cousins, however, knew that Mahmood was stubborn, and that he would not be ordered around or threatened. 'He must be helping them to safety,' Nadira said to Dahlia, when she was sure my mother could not hear. 'How like Mahmood.' And it was like my father. But the morning turned into afternoon, and there was still no word. My mother continued to weep. She could not know that her husband had, three times, passed within two hundred yards of Nana's house in his doubling-back attempts to confuse any informers and stool-pigeons who might be trailing him. If she had, she would have run out on to the streets, hurling herself on the bonnet of the car.

Towards the middle of the afternoon, just as the family from downstairs was finally assembling at the safe-house in Mohakhali, the silent baby in its swaddling began to stir and warble, and to screw its ugly face up into a ball. My mother made no response, and soon I began to cry properly. It had been some hours since I was fed, and I probably needed to be changed as well. My mother, so sunk in herself, still made no response.

'Shiri!' my grandmother called. 'Shiri, wake up and pay attention. Your baby is crying.'

'Shall I take him?' Mira said. 'Shall I take dear little Saadi? He is only a little bit cross, and perhaps he could be hungry, too. He has been so good.'

'No,' my grandmother said. 'Shiri, you must take care of him. Get up and make an effort, now – this is not like you at all.'

'She thinks Mahmood will be caught out in the streets when the curfew falls,' Era said, in a low voice.

'How could he?' Sharmin said. 'Causing everyone such worry like this.'

'Causing everyone such worry – oh, that is so much like

214

Mahmood,' Era said. 'He would never consider what other people are thinking about, or worrying over. He just does what he thinks is the right thing to do.'

'A very annoying trait in a person,' Sharmin said, keeping her voice down.

'What is that noise?' said one of the great-grandmothers, awakening like me from her sleep.

'Poor little Saadi,' my grandmother said. She got up from her chair, shuffled and cast her shawl over her shoulder, and went over to my basket. She picked me up; with a baby's instinct for the unexpected, I began to cry with new force. Finally, my mother roused herself; she sat up, uncovered her face, and took me from her mother. Soon, as if through the repetition of routine alone, I had quietened down, and was feeding contentedly.

'What was that noise?' Nana said. He had come through from his study at the front of the house. Even in the current state of overcrowding, it was understood that he must have his own undisturbed space. His daughters and grandchildren and mothers and cousins might colonize the rest of the house, invading even the servants' annexe, resting the whole day in the salon, finding corners in which to pass the time with small-scale near-silent activities like paan-grinding, embroidery, sock-darning, pickle-bottling and the like. But Nana must have his retreat in his depleted library, and when he came out, the daughters and the little awestruck cousins busied themselves, knowing that something must have disturbed him.

'It is dear little Saadi,' Nani said. 'He was just hungry and woke up. Poor little thing, he can't tell us that he wants something other than by crying. But he's quite all right now.'

'Can't he be kept quiet with the other children?' Nana said.

'Mary can't keep him quiet with *The Snow Queen*,' Shiri said. Her face was red with weeping; she did not turn to her father when she spoke, but kept herself hunched over the baby. 'The other children will listen to stories or play games, but he's too little to understand any of that. Poor little mite.'

215

'Poor little mite,' said Era.

'He must keep quiet,' Nana said. 'We mustn't be heard from the street by anyone who passes.' His eyes went round the room, to his seven daughters, one upstairs, to his daughter-in-law and three female cousins; perhaps he thought, too, a dreadful thought, of a tableau; his wife and mothers and perhaps even the grand-daughters, too. The mind shrank from it. I was the youngest child in the house, and the only child of an age to cry incontinently, who could not understand what the situation was. My wails could be heard in the street, when I cried, and to the passing soldiery, it would be like the display of a rebel flag, a reason for forcing an entry.

'Poor little Saadi,' Mira said. 'He can't be expected to under-stand what's happening. We can't tell him not to cry, he wouldn't listen.'

'That's so,' my grandfather said, considering. His lawyer's logical brain went through various considerations. 'He must never be left alone, that's all. Carry him about with you – not just his mother, but the rest of you girls, too, take turns. If he wants to sleep, put him down but don't leave him. And have cake to hand at all times. If it begins to look as if he might be thinking of crying – beginning to look like that, no more – then distract him, feed him, interest him, jiggle him. He mustn't cry. Give him cake and mishti doi. Babies like that. He must be allowed to eat what-ever he likes.'

And that is how I was allowed to eat whatever I liked, without any restraint at all. There was no shortage of mishti doi, it being made in the kitchen rather than bought in from confectioners. From that moment onwards, my aunts took turns looking after me. I grew popular with them because a baby cared for at every minute, whose every need is anticipated and fulfilled before he has even begun to express it, is a placid and cheerful baby, as well as a very fat one. My aunts said they loved my chubby face; they loved my cheerful demeanour. They passed me from one to another with some regret, looking forward to their next turn looking after

Saadi. Anyone who came into the house would have seen me being cradled in an aunt's elbow as she crooned to me – Era, Sharmin, Mary, Nadira, Mira, Dahlia, even Bubbly, though she was no more than thirteen and, I was told in later years, not very good at it.

On the table or the armrest of a chair by them was a terracotta pot of mishti doi, a teaspoon stuck in it, and from time to time, not interrupting her burble of conversation or under-the-breath song, the aunt of the moment would lean forward, dig into the pot and bring another half-teaspoon to my little wrinkled mouth. In the whole of that time, I hardly had the opportunity to cry. No sooner, day or night, had my face begun to move inwards and my brow to furrow than an aunt moved in and embarked on a well-established routine of Saadi-distracting, involving the pulling of funny faces, jogging up and down, a favourite knitted rabbit, tickling on the tummy (mine) and the regular administration of half-teaspoons of mishti doi.

It is a sign of how desperate and serious those months of 1971 were that the other children in the house had no resentment or complaint against this exceptional treatment of a baby. They never produced, as far as I can discover, that universal childhood complaint, 'It isn't fair,' when they saw the constant watching and concern that I was attracting. They knew that it wasn't fair, none of it, even the very smallest of them. I slept contentedly, in an atmosphere of love, from the March curfew until the day in December that Bangla Desh was liberated, and I did not cry. The house in Dhanmondi was as quiet as a tomb, and no soldier was drawn by his curiosity in a baby crying to force the gates and enter.

But this is to move ahead in the story.

9.

'What is that?' my mother said.

'What is what?' Nadira said.

'That sound,' my mother said. They all listened. In the city, far away, a noise like a howl was rising. It was what they had all been dreading. Two days before, nobody had known what the sound had meant. It was a siren, driven about the streets of the old city, of Sadarghat, Gulistan, Dhanmondi, Mohakhali and the other parts of the city, in warning; it signified, a radio announcement had made clear, the beginning of a curfew. Now it was one o'clock, and the sirens were sounding. There had still been no word from my father. He was out there in the city somewhere. Nobody had the heart to tell my mother that he must have returned, in safety, to the house in Elephant Road – that her husband was a sensible man who would not risk his life in this way.

'Put the radio on,' Era said, and Nadira hastened to do so. The new audio cabinet, a stylish model in teak, included a radio. These days, it was kept permanently tuned to Radio Calcutta, which could be trusted.

The news ran through the events in Dacca and in the rest of the country. Universities had been burnt; intellectuals rounded up. There was no news of Sheikh Mujib. There were international condemnations. The curfew had been imposed and had been lifted for five hours during the day before being put in place again. Finally, the radio news regretted to announce the death of Begum Sufiya Kemal, in unknown circumstances—

'Oh,' Nani said.

'How could they?' Nadira said; her eyes began to fill with tears. Sufiya lived so close; the whole family knew her; they had been to her house many times. How could they?

'But all she did was to write some poems,' Mira said. 'How can they shoot women for writing poems?'

And Begum Sufiya would be remembered, above all, the radio continued, for poems that encouraged her countrymen and -women in the struggle for freedom. There was a brief pause, and another voice began to read a poem. It was Sufiya's voice; the poem must have been recorded at some time, and the recording

218

obtained somehow by Radio Calcutta. '"This is no time to be braiding your hair,"' the poem began.

'My friend's poem,' Nana said. 'I am glad they are letting her read this.' He had been called through from his study by the sound of poetry, or by the sound of his friend's voice on the radio. But he had not heard the news.

'She has been killed, Papa,' Nadira said.

'How has she been killed?' Nana said.

'They didn't say,' Nani said. 'Only that she has died. How could they?'

'They wouldn't,' Nana said. 'They wouldn't dare. We would have heard if she had been killed. This is a mistake, I know. She could not be dead.'

'The radio said that she is dead,' Nani said, with surprise.

'The radio is mistaken,' Nana said. 'Where is Mahmood? The curfew has begun now.'

And the strange thing was that Nana was right. Sufiya was not dead at all. The announcement on Radio Calcutta of her passing was mistaken, and taken from unreliable information. A street or two away, Sufiya and her daughters were sitting, just as my family was, inside, waiting for news, and she had the shock of hearing her own death announced, and then of listening to her own voice reading her famous poem. Three days later, my grandfather had the pleasure of reading an advertisement in the newspaper, placed there by Sufiya herself, in which she announced to all her friends that, contrary to reports, she was alive and well, and hoping to be listened to for many years to come. There was something steely and full of reprimand about the tone of the advert. Nobody could doubt that it was Sufiya herself who had written it, and there were no rumours about her having met her death from that point onwards.

In the street, the sirens howled like cats. Beyond that, there was no sound. 'Mahmood must be safely inside,' Era said. 'He has taken shelter. He will come tomorrow. Shiri, he is sensible, your husband.'

'I know he is dead,' my mother said. She gulped and clutched the gold hem of her sari. 'How could he – how could he go to the help of those people downstairs? We hardly know them.'

'He did what he had to do,' my grandfather said. It was so conclusive, the tone in which he said it, that the music of its serious finality drew the children from upstairs; they stood, lined up along the banisters, and gazed, shocked, at the adults giving way.

My sisters were the last to take their positions: they had been concealing themselves on the front balcony of the house, watching from behind a chair the distant fires of the city and the silent, empty street. They wondered, as they stood, why the aunts and cousins and the rest of the grown-ups were crying and silent. Surely their father would put things to rights when he came, as he would come. As he was coming, in fact. They had seen him hurrying along from a hundred yards away, hunched under the trees, swift and surreptitious, but, to his children, an unmistakable walk and silhouette. It was strange that he had not made an effort to arrive before the sirens started sounding but, after all, he was not so very late. In the past, he had often arrived twenty or thirty minutes late for dinner at Nana's house, kept behind at the office. It was ridiculous to make such a fuss when he was only five or ten minutes late for lunch. And before Sushmita, in her practical way, could say something to point this out, the gates at the front of the house were clanging open and shut; the grown-ups were rising to their feet; the light footfalls of Pa were heard in the glass-fronted side porch of the house, and there he was.

He looked tired and untidy; his jacket was over the crook of his arm. He was a little late, but he had had things to do all day, and sometimes things take longer to achieve than people anticipate and, after all, he was only six or seven minutes late. Sushmita and Sunchita were glad to see their father, but not excessively so. After all, everyone had been expecting his arrival, all morning, and here he was.

It was a surprise to them when Nana strode forward out of his chair, took their father by his thin shoulders and shook him hard. There were not many occasions on which Grandfather raised his voice; perhaps this one was the first one they would remember. He shouted into my father's face: 'Do not do that! Never again do that to my daughter! Never, ever, do that to my wife, or to me, or to my daughters! Never, ever, do that to my grandchildren!' My grandfather went on through the table of affinities. It was as if he were attempting to run through all the possibilities of insult and offence and the vulnerable. His rage took three or four sentences to lower from its highest pitch, as he remembered the need to remain quiet; after twenty seconds, the rage continued at a lower volume. Into my father's face my grandfather shouted, a mute in his throat but no restraint on his rage.

Sunchita and Sushmita watched, horrified and appalled, at the unknown sight of their grandfather shouting; the still less imaginable sight of their father taking the abuse. From any unjustified display of power their father, they knew, would walk away. Now he had arrived ten minutes later than he should have, and not only was Grandfather shouting at him, but Father was standing there accepting the abuse, as long as it seemed to go on.

My aunts and my mother, drying her tears and coming to her husband, found this a less unfamiliar sight than the children. They remembered the last time Nana had burst out shouting. It had been fourteen years before. It had been the day that Boro-mama had run away, leaving the garden path unswept; the day he had run away to marry Sharmin, who was now sitting in a placid way in a corner of the salon, keeping an eye on their four children. (She was glad to see her brother-in-law Mahmood: she had never really doubted that he would get here safely, and she went on knitting.) That was the last time Nana had shouted, when he had raised his voice and demanded the immediate attendance of Era, who had known all about it. My grandfather never lost his temper, and never raised his voice. He must have shouted as a boy, though it was hard to imagine. But in family stories, these were the two

221

occasions when he raised his voice: to Era, when she knew all about Laddu's elopement; and to Mahmood, the day he came in after the curfew had been declared, making his wife cry. For the rest of his life, my grandfather never saw anything to make him shout. But that day, he did shout, and my father knew he was right to.

10: The Song the Flower Sang

1.

Between March and December 1971, the war of independence continued. The course of that war has been told by other people, many times, and so has the story of the hundreds of thousands of people who were killed. In December, the Indian government came in on the side of Sheikh Mujib's liberation fighters, and within a few days, an independent Bangla Desh was declared.

For those eight months, all Nana's family lived in the house in Dhanmondi. The domestic arrangements were complex, but they worked quite efficiently. Boro-mama and his family had a room to themselves, as did we; the great-grandmothers shared with two aunts, and the doubling-up went on in quite a sensible way. There had been talk of abandoning Dacca to go into the country but, in fact, that proved much more dangerous for many people. Millions of people, especially Hindus, had fled to India at the outbreak of trouble. But we did not do that. My grandfather had great faith in the idea that the worst trouble would not happen if he was certain enough that it would not happen. He faced down catastrophe. And perhaps he felt that he and Nani had suffered enough when they were young, living in Calcutta, and their eldest boy had been killed at fifteen by a Japanese bomb in the air-raids. Nothing afterwards could ever be as bad as that. And, strangely enough, nothing afterwards ever was as bad. They came through that terrible time, when the violence and terror washed up against the gate of the house, but no further. They survived, and were still there at the other end.

Nani had a strong emotion afterwards about this time. She was not exactly nostalgic about it, but in later years, when I was old enough to be placed next to Nana at dinner and be called Churchill, she would often mention this time. 'Do you remember,' she would say, her leg resting on the teak footrest, 'do you remember the steamed rui that Sharmin taught Ahmed how to make when everyone was living here, all through 'seventy-one? Do you remember, Bubbly? It was so good, that steamed rui, with lemon and ginger. And she taught him, and he never got it right afterwards. I don't know why. But it was never so delicious ever again. He didn't listen properly, or he made some changes of his own, wretched boy, and completely spoilt the dish. Oh, I loved to eat that steamed rui. I could have eaten it every day.'

'It was so clever of her,' Bubbly would say. She loved the details of food as much as Nani did – she could remember, years later, the exact sequence of dishes she had eaten at her sisters' weddings, recalling them in loving detail. 'Because of course there was not always a great choice of things to eat, that year, but you could often get rui when there was no other fish to be had. And we all simply loved it. I could eat it now, in fact.' She turned to a brother-in-law and began to explain the details of the steamed fish. He was a journalist; he often expressed surprise when, unlike most families, his wife's family's memories of the 1971 war of independence revolved around the dishes they had eaten, all summer long. 'I wish Sharmin would come back and teach Ahmed how to make it again, but she says she can't remember, and she says she doesn't know what's wrong with the way Ahmed cooks it, so that would really be a fool's errand.'

It was not a happy time, of course not. But it was the time when all Nana's family were about him, and nobody in his family circle met their end that summer, through some miracle.

At the very end of the year, when Bangla Desh was declared, Nana gathered his family around him. Rustum came in from the garden, and he had been asked to bring a sledgehammer with him. Preceding my grandfather and grandmother and everyone, Rustum opened the cellar door – the one anyone would have thought was a cupboard in the hallway, no more than that, and went downstairs to the oddly small cellar. The whole family could not fit in the cellar as it had been reconstructed, and the aunts and some of the children crowded up the wooden staircase. Outside, the two great-grandmothers, Nana's mothers, were asking each other what it was that could be going on, what he was up to now. At the top of the stairs, underneath the single lightbulb that illuminated the space, was my elder sister Sushmita, holding me up to watch Rustum's dramatic gesture. I gazed, bewildered, not knowing what Sushmita was pointing at.

But Rustum raised his sledgehammer, and struck at exactly the right point in the wall. He knew exactly where he should strike. There was a crack; he raised the hammer again, and struck again, and the thin plaster gave way. Behind the half-inch-thick layer, crates of books, of paintings, a harmonium could be seen. It was three years since the library and other treasures had been sealed up. Nadira came forward and pulled at the plaster; now the wall had been broached, it could just be pulled apart with bare hands. And then Boro-mama joined in, and Pultoo; in no time the secret library was there, and everyone was choking in a cloud of plaster dust. There was a cry at the top of the stairs. It was my sister, Sushmita. 'I couldn't help it,' she said. 'I dropped Saadi.' It was true. She had dropped me on my bottom, and I sat at the top of the stairs, wailing. It was a novel experience. For the first time, nobody rushed to stop me making that awful noise. 'I just couldn't help it,' she said. 'He's just – he's just so *fat*.' Everyone looked at me, and saw that she was quite right; Mary and Dahlia, at the bottom of the stairs, began to giggle helplessly. Months of feeding, of keeping me quiet with mishti doi, had produced a gargantuan infant. My eyes were deeply buried in fat rolls of cheek, like currants in a bun.

'Something must be done about that,' Nana said, quite seriously.

And then Nadira played a song.

225

2.

But other people had a different sort of time, during those months.

Mrs Khandekar's sons were constant attenders at the student rallies, the protest meetings that were an almost daily occurrence in the first months of 1971. They came home only to eat, bringing friends and fellow revolutionaries. Mrs Khandekar took to ordering large quantities of food for dinner, knowing that twelve very hungry people might arrive without warning. They sat about the dinner table with their wild hair, bringing a new atmosphere into the house, having the kind of argument that consists of everyone agreeing very energetically. They would sleep – the boys in their old rooms, the others in spare rooms, or, if there were too many, on sofas, however they could manage themselves. And then, in the morning, they would be gone, off to make their feelings felt at another rally.

The younger of the sons of Mrs Khandekar had begun to smoke in this wild-eyed, impassioned company. She had once made him promise that he would never smoke. But there were other reasons for her to worry about him, these days.

The two boys came to her, and said that they were leaving Dacca to prepare for the struggle to come. She muted her feelings. She understood why she could not know where they were. But it was hard for her.

When my grandfather came to see the Khandekars, to ask their advice, he did not know that in the kitchen, waiting to see Mrs Khandekar, was a man called Altaf. Altaf sat with the Khandekar servants and Rustum, my grandfather's driver, listening to their conversation but not contributing much. My grandfather left, and actually saw Altaf. But he did not recognize him as a musician who had played at many parties in the past, and he did not wonder what Altaf might be doing there.

When my grandfather had left, Mr Khandekar went to his study, and Altaf followed Mrs Khandekar into the pink sitting room with the chairs of green silk. It was the place he had first met Mrs Khandekar and talked to her about his problems, before she had solved them.

'Thank you for coming,' Mrs Khandekar said. 'I do hope there were no difficulties reaching us. Do put that down – I'm not expecting you to play today.'

Altaf put his harmonium in its case down. He wondered why Mrs Khandekar had asked him to bring it, if it were not to be played. And it could be the cause of suspicion, to carry a musical instrument through the streets, these days.

'Mrs Khandekar-aunty,' Altaf said boldly. 'I thank you for your every kindness to me.'

'We all live in hard times,' Mrs Khandekar said. 'I know that there was nothing you could have done about the change in circumstances. I could not take advantage of you because of something that you did not foresee.'

Since Amit's departure, Mrs Khandekar had agreed to let Altaf stay in the apartment in Old Dacca on his own, only asking him to go on paying the half of the rent that he had been paying. She understood, she had said, the situation. She had suggested at first that Altaf would not need to pay the full amount until he had found somebody else to share the flat with. But – with a shrug – there was no particular hurry for that. 'We are not,' Mrs Khandekar had said, 'living in normal times.'

Altaf was grateful for this. When Mrs Khandekar, a week later, sent him a note asking him to meet her in the English cemetery at a certain time, he did so. She had handed him a letter – a thick envelope, containing a long letter, and perhaps, Altaf thought, some wedges of banknotes, too. As they walked from one end of the cemetery to the other, they could have been a son and his mother. The decaying tombs, overgrown with creepers and grass, were little visited, and kept only by a sad old custodian at the gate, who did not care who they were. Most people were kept away by the fear of snakes breeding in the thick, undisturbed growth; a fear Altaf rather shared as Mrs Khandekar strode through the knee-deep vegetation. She had given him the address of a house in Azimpur. Altaf agreed to take the package there that afternoon.

He understood very well what Mrs Khandekar was asking of him, and he understood why it was him that she had asked. These days, Mrs Khandekar was followed when she left the house; if she had something to take to another address, that house would be watched, too. Altaf was not important enough to be watched. He was not an obvious part of Mrs Khandekar's life. So she passed him an envelope containing hundreds of rupees, and asked him to deliver it to a house in Azimpur. He had no idea who the people in the house in Azimpur could be.

Since then, he had done the same thing twice more for Mrs Khandekar. Once she had asked him to bring a tiffin pail – the ordinary steel three-tiered sort that everyone had – and on a bench in Baldha Gardens in the shade of a red-flowering tree, they had unobtrusively swapped. She walked off with his, and he took hers to another house, behind a wall in Minto Street. She had given him the address. It was strangely heavy, that tiffin pail. Something thudded about inside it, something weighty. It seemed to be padded with cotton wool, or wrapped in muslin, or something of that sort. Mrs Khandekar on the next occasion had been meticulous about giving him back his own pail, the one she had taken away with her, washed. But that had been two weeks afterwards, and Altaf had by then bought a replacement tiffin pail. They were not expensive items, and he was grateful to Mrs Khandekar for other things.

He was not a fool. He understood that the Khandekar boys had gone away, like many students of that age. He himself had been to a meeting of tens, perhaps hundreds of thousands, at the racecourse where Sheikh Mujib had read a speech, and Sufiya Kamal had recited a poem. He had felt pride that in the past he had played at her house, and had been listened to by him. Many people who had attended such meetings were preparing to fight. It was to those people that he was conveying Mrs Khandekar's packages. Or, rather, it was to people who knew those people that his deliveries were being made. These houses were the first of a chain, in a sequence, and at the end of it, perhaps, were the Khandekar boys, who had responded to the times by retreating, and preparing to fight. Others, like Amit, were preparing for the war to come in their own way, by running away to India. He pushed the thought down as unworthy of himself. He had heard from Amit only once, in a letter that was not long, from Calcutta, where he was safe. There had been no return address: perhaps Amit had overlooked it, or perhaps he thought there was no point in giving one. He said he was moving from address to address at the moment, living on the kindness of friends.

In the pink-and-green sitting room, Mrs Khandekar made tense conversation of a neutral sort. Was it true that the Hindu family in the courtyard house across the road from Altaf's had moved away? How sad. And the children who lived opposite, they must be quite large now – ten, the girl must be? Time went so quickly, it was as if it were yesterday that she was born. Time was not going quickly in Mrs Khandekar's sitting room. She did not call for tea, perhaps because Altaf had already had his tea in the kitchen. Finally she stood up and went to the sideboard, bent down and pulled out a rosewood case from underneath. Altaf recognized it, in general terms: it was the case of a harmonium, another one. But it obviously contained much more than a harmonium, from the way Mrs Khandekar was struggling to lift it. She put it by his chair and sat down again on her sofa.

'It would be so kind of you to take this to a dear friend of mine,' she said. 'He lent it to me, and I think I need to take it back to him. I would ask the servants, but . . .'

No reason seemed to come to Mrs Khandekar's mind for not asking the servants to deliver it. But Altaf understood perfectly well.

'Take a motor-rickshaw,' Mrs Khandekar said. 'Take two, one after the other. You know what I mean. You can leave your instrument here. It will be quite safe, and I will ask someone to bring it back to you this afternoon – no, tomorrow, if that isn't an inconvenience. Here is some money – I do hope it isn't inconvenient.'

She gave him the address – a place deep in Armanitola, not far from where Altaf lived – and she stood up to say goodbye. He lifted the case: it was heavy. There was no harmonium inside it, he believed. He left the house, trying to carry the harmonium as if it were of normal weight; as if it were the case he had arrived with. He did not see anyone observing him, and certainly it would be hard for them to be sure whether Altaf had entered the house with a harmonium or not. He wondered if Mrs Khandekar had decided on a harmonium because she thought Altaf would carry it naturally, being accustomed to it; or perhaps she had not given the matter that degree of thought, and it was simply something conveniently to hand, very much like an object that she could ask him to bring, like the tiffin pails they had swapped on a previous meeting. In any case, he walked down the leafy Dhanmondi street in a brisk way. The pavement cobbler with his last and his tools, settled in the shade of a tree, looked up as he passed; the security guard outside another house, sitting on a chipped wooden chair, fanning himself with a newspaper, greeted him in a bored manner, saying, 'Good morning, brother.' It was hard to know whether anyone else was observing or following him, but Altaf thought not. For some years, it had been deemed suspicious to walk the streets of Dacca with a musical instrument. Mrs Khandekar had overlooked that, and the harmonium case must have been exactly the right size for whatever it now contained.

At the corner of the street, he hailed a green motor-rickshaw. He told the driver to go to Armanitola, and the driver unhooked the cage that closed in the passenger seat. Altaf would not haggle over the fare today. 'Musician, are you?' the driver said, as they set off, and Altaf agreed that he was. 'You know my favourite song?' the driver said, and began to hum 'Amar Shonar Bangla', the Tagore song. You could be arrested for that, but neither of them seemed to care, and in a moment Altaf joined in. Around them the sound of the traffic rose, and the leaden scents of the busy street. Through the noise of hooting and the grinding sound of gear changes, none of the patriotic song could be heard. 'My golden Bengal,' Altaf and the driver sang quietly, and they could have been holding a conversation about anything, there in the motor-rickshaw.

The rickshaw dropped him two streets away from the address Mrs Khandekar had given him – in the end, the driver abandoned his brotherly gesture and, since Altaf had not named his price at the beginning, charged him twice over. Altaf walked in the opposite direction to the address he was seeking; dived inside a shop and then immediately out again; cut down an alley, and another, emerging in the main street; crossed the road and back again; and finally, through making reversals and cut-throughs, delaying and hurrying, he found himself at the blue-painted, rusty gate of the house. He banged on the gate, and quickly it was opened by a young man, his hair wild, his chin stubbled with a dusting of white; he wore round, wire-framed spectacles. To Altaf's surprise, the stranger embraced him before pulling him inside and closing

231

the gate. 'We are old friends, you see, brother,' the man said. 'Now come inside. You need to wait for an hour before leaving.'

That was the fourth time Altaf had taken something at Mrs Khandekar's request to another part of the city. There were half a dozen addresses he made these deliveries to. He never knew where these packages went after he had passed them on, or who had given Mrs Khandekar six hand-guns and boxes of ammunition in a harmonium case – for example – to pass on to the freedom fighters who were already taking their positions by the beginning of March 1971.

3.

The rains were heavy that year. Mrs Khandekar's younger son was in the country in August, with a small group of commandos. He did not know exactly where – it was somewhere near Tangail. The country was quiet, undeveloped, and very wet. It came to them as grey, through a dense veil of monsoon.

Somewhere about there were Pakistani troops. A week before, and forty miles away, the commandos had had a success. Word had reached them that a Pakistani convoy would arrive in the district on a certain day. They had taken up positions in a ditch by the side of the road. They had endured three hours of rain and knee-high water, but then the convoy had come. They had hurled grenades into the lorries, and fired on the fleeing Pakistani soldiers. It was a successful operation. The commandos had swiftly moved south.

None of the commandos knew whether there were any Pakistani troops in the district. The villagers said there were. But they had rarely met anyone in their lives who did not come from the vicinity of Tangail. That might just have meant that they had met friendly commandos who talked Bengali with a Dacca accent. But the order had come to move southwards after the successful assault on the Pakistani convoy, and to reconnoitre the situation there.

So they stayed where they were, in the country east of Tangail, until further orders.

The elder son of Mrs Khandekar had known of better platoons. Manju, who had joined them three weeks before to direct the operation, had made it clear. His previous body of men had had enough tents, straw mattresses, plates to eat off, and even, he said, pillows. They had erected bamboo cottages to sleep in, with dry floors even in the monsoon. This platoon had only three tents for ten men, slept on the ground and ate off leaves or even fragments of artillery shells. Added to that was the discomfort of the monsoon. The elder son of Mrs Khandekar had not worn dry clothes for weeks. His skin itched constantly, all over. On his forearms, the sparks from the sten gun had raised blisters, which had become infected. Manju pointed out that they were Bengalis. They knew about the monsoon. They could live in rain for weeks on end, and it would be helping troops elsewhere to travel by boat and to swim. The Pakistani soldiers came from a dry country, and would be suffering far more than they were. They did not know what to do with water.

The elder son of Mrs Khandekar was the platoon's quartermaster. He obtained food for the men. For weeks now, they had eaten nothing but vegetables, lentils and rice. It was what villagers lived on, and what they could supply. Sometimes, for breakfast, there was nothing to be had but jackfruit. The elder son of Mrs Khandekar had half a dozen farmers and merchants in the district from whom he bought food; he circulated around them irregularly, coming at different times of day. He did not believe that his contacts would have informed on him to the Pakistanis, if there were any in the district. But there was no point in taking risks. Like all the others, he ate the vegetables, rice and lentils. They drank water from the ponds when they could find no well, and cooked the food in old, battered pots which made everything taste of mud. Once, he had eaten chicken from clean white plates, inside, in a warm room.

One of the farmers had told him that there was a big old house a mile or so beyond the ponds. He had never gone so far, but

233

in the interests of making his movements unpredictable, had set off there one day, shortly before dawn. Those old houses where the zamindars had lived often had substantial stores of food. If the owner was sympathetic, they might even be able to move into a room or two. He trudged along the roads, the water coming down hard. It muted everything but the smells of the country, rich and earthy; the colours of the early morning dulled in the downpour, and there was no sound but the steady hiss of rain. Underfoot, the roads were brown and soft. The stream of water down the back of his neck was constant, as it had been for weeks.

The zamindar's house loomed up like a mirage in the rain. 'The first thing you'll see,' the farmer had said, 'is the mosque on the zamindar's land.' It was an old pink-and-white building, on the far side of a fishing lake. It was small, even for a village mosque, no more than twenty feet long, set against the walls of the zamindar's land. The elder son of Mrs Khandekar walked round the lake. In the gardens of the house, he could see an enormous rain tree – it must have been hundreds of years old. In the branches, the shrieks of parakeets were audible over the sound of the rain, and there was the nest of some huge bird, perhaps a fish eagle. There seemed to be nobody about. The gate to the property was hanging open, as if the house had been abandoned. He went inside the grounds. By the mosque was a walled grave-yard – the final resting places of the zamindar's family. He knew these places: it was where the family came home to, in the end.

The house was a single long building, painted red, and had not been lived in for some time. The windows were hanging open, and the curtains soaked with the rain. The front entrance had no door. But there were signs of habitation – a window frame at the left side of the house was blackened, suggesting that a fire had been lit within without care, probably just on the floor of the house. The elder son of Mrs Khandekar decided not to approach the house from the front. He scuttled along the inside of the garden wall, underneath the great tree, and quickly he was behind the house. He could see now that it had once been larger: the stone flags running at a right angle from the main body of the house suggested it had once had two wings. Behind the house there was a pretty old gazebo. It was properly roofed, and its pillars were covered with blue-and-white porcelain mosaics. The elder son of Mrs Khandekar looked at the solid brick flooring with envy. After weeks of sleeping in a tent in the mud, he had not yet allowed himself to consider a bed with soft, clean white sheets. But the idea of sleeping on solid, clean dry bricks filled him with longing. Beyond the gazebo, there was an orchard; two lines of old fruit trees. They were huge old mango trees, guava trees and, the elder son of Mrs Khandekar could see, a lychee tree. That last one was covered with a net against bats – he knew that the bats always get to lychees first, unless you shield them. But the net was ripped and full of holes: it must have been abandoned for two, perhaps three years.

In the rain, the orchard seemed enchanted, hanging weightlessly behind a veil. The elder son of Mrs Khandekar forgot his errand; he did not care that there was no food to be had in an abandoned

'The monsoon broke, and then the next day Nadira was born. A monsoon baby is the best,' Era said.

'No, you're wrong,' Mary said. 'You aren't remembering properly. Nadira was born and the monsoon broke the next day. Everyone was sitting about, fanning themselves, cursing the heat, waiting for the rains to come, and then there was Nadira instead. When it rained the next day, everybody said it would be good for the baby in its first days. It is so easy to make those kinds of confusion.'

'Sister,' Era said, 'I remember perfectly. I remember the doctor coming through the gate in Rankin Street with his bag, and struggling with his bag and an umbrella at the same time. You must remember that.'

'No, sister,' Mary said. 'The important detail—'

'The important detail is the doctor, struggling with his umbrella, and the rains beginning. Shiri, don't you remember?'

My mother spread her hands wide, smiling. 'When you say the circumstances, Era, it sounds as if that is how it happened. But then Mary has a story, which sounds to me as if that is the real story. I was there, I know that. And I know that some years the rains break before Nadira's birthday, and sometimes after; and I remember being at home in Rankin Street, and it raining so hard outside, and there was a baby in the house, crying so loud. But it could have been Mira, or it could have been Nadira. I think you will have to ask Big-brother.'

'Where is Big-brother?' Dahlia said. 'He is coming, isn't he? And Sharmin?'

'Yes, yes,' Nadira said. 'Don't fret. Everyone is coming. Do I look—'

'Stop asking that, all the time,' my mother said. 'You look perfect. Don't play with your hair and don't keep touching your face in that nervous way, and everything will be just perfect.'

'You will come and visit me?' Nadira said. 'When we go to live in England? In Sheffield?'

'We will do our very best,' Dahlia said. 'It is such a long way. And it won't be for ever that you go.'

'Please, try to come,' Nadira said. 'I want you to come, all of you.'

'Do you remember when Shiri went to Barisal?' Mary said. 'After she got married? I don't know why, but none of us ever went to see her. It was just such a long way to go, and at the end of it, there was just Barisal. Did we come to visit you, Shiri?'

'Well,' my mother said, 'I think Mira was planning to come and visit, but then, as things turned out, I came home in any case. I don't remember why Mira wanted to come and visit. I don't think anyone asked her to. But she wrote a letter saying she was hoping to come and stay, and then, of course, Mahmood became very concerned, and wondered whether we had enough furniture to entertain a guest. It was a strange thing to wonder, because when we moved into that house in Barisal there was nothing but furniture in it – the rooms just filled up with furniture from all the neighbours that none of them wanted. It took us weeks to clear it away and find somewhere else to store it. And then Mira's letter arrived and Mahmood became concerned that he would have to go and find a bed and a chair and a table and all those things that guests seem to need.'

'And then I didn't come after all,' Mira said.

'No, that's so,' my mother said. 'It wasn't your fault, truly, though. I think you would have come if I hadn't come home again. I don't know why you wanted to come. I kept saying in my letters how beastly Barisal was. I'm sure it wasn't really. I'm sure if you went back there it would be just a place like any other. But you know how things were.'

'We thought you were just being polite,' Era said. 'I thought you were saying those things about Barisal because you thought, if you pretended it was lovely, we would all feel that we had no excuse for not coming to visit. We thought you were putting us off as visitors.'

'But Mira wanted to come anyway,' my mother said sensibly.

'Please come to Sheffield,' Nadira said, her eyes big and frightened. 'I don't know what I would do if I thought I wasn't going to—'

'Nadira, don't you start crying,' Mira said. 'If you start crying, we are just going to start all over again.'

'I'm not going to cry,' Nadira said. 'And there is the first car. I think it's the first car, isn't it?'

9.

Pultoo had organized all the children, and half a dozen cousins, to stand at the door of the hotel where Iqtiar and Nadira were to marry. The hotel reception halls were hung with garlands, and decorated under Pultoo's direction: banners, flowers, lamps, bowls of water with water-lilies floating in them; he had even cleverly veiled some of the lights with coloured cellophane to warm up the light in the room. At the door, his nieces and nephews and cousins and cousins' children were leaping up and down with excitement. The rest of Nadira's family had gone inside, and it was only for Pultoo and his gang of merry pranksters to carry out the last act of Pultoo's meticulous plot. In each hand, all of the gang held a shoe. They were Iqtiar's shoes, and Pultoo had stolen every last one of them.

The night before, one of Iqtiar's brothers had let Pultoo into their house after everyone had gone to bed. The same brother, who had been told all about the prank, had managed to remove not just Iqtiar's wedding shoes, but every pair of shoes Iqtiar owned from the bridegroom's room. Pultoo had brought a sack, and the seven pairs of shoes had gone into it before he had fled. Behind him, Iqtiar's brother was covering his mouth and trying not to laugh.

Now, all fourteen shoes were in the hands of Pultoo's gang. 'Remember,' Pultoo said to us. 'He doesn't get them back – not a single shoe – without paying us the ransom money. Do you understand, Saadi?'

'Yes, yes,' I said. 'I understand, Choto-mama. He doesn't get his old shoe back from me.'

Choto-mama had asked me the question because I was the smallest of the conspirators, and the one most likely to forget what I was supposed to do and hand the shoe over if Iqtiar-uncle asked politely. But Choto-mama underestimated me. I was going to hang on for dear life.

And then, on the other side of the glass doors of the hotel, the cars of Iqtiar and his family drew up. His father and uncles, his cousins, sisters, brothers – including the brother who had been Pultoo's co-conspirator – came into the hotel, laughing. We could see why: every one of them was wearing shoes, except for Iqtiar, coming in last. He was barefoot, and looking very serious.

'You see,' Iqtiar's brother explained later, 'Iqtiar knew that Pultoo was going to steal his wedding shoes. He told us two days before. He said that he didn't care – that if Pultoo stole the wedding shoes, he was going to wear his best shoes anyway. He did not reckon on two things. The first was that one of the culprits was in the room, and in his own family. Namely, me. The second was that the pranksters had set their hearts on stealing not just the wedding shoes he had bought for the express purpose. We were planning to steal all his shoes, altogether.

'Well, when he woke, and started getting dressed, it did not take him long to understand that all his shoes were gone. So he said to me, "Who takes the same size in shoes as I do, bhai?" And I had to admit that I did. So he said, "Give me your shoes, bhai." "I am not giving you these shoes," I said. "I am wearing these shoes, to your wedding, you fool." "Well, give me your best shoes," he said. "I have sent them away to be cleaned," I said. "Well, your second-best shoes," he said. "The sole is detached, and the heel has come off," I said. "Then your third-best shoes," he said. "Alas," I said. "Those too have been stolen by the pranksters. They must have mistaken my third-best shoes

288

for your best pair." "Then give me your fourth-best shoes," he said, in a fit of rage. "My fourth-best shoes?" I said. "Your fourth-best shoes," he said. "I have lent my fourth-best shoes to Grandmother," I said. "She finds them very comfortable." "Is there nobody else in this family who can lend me a pair of shoes?" Iqtiar-brother then shouted out. But answer came there none.'

I had been nominated by the gang to negotiate a price for the return of Iqtiar's shoes. I was the youngest, and that was my task. I was pushed to the front. In my hand, I was gripping one of the wedding shoes. Pultoo had thoroughly briefed me in what I was to say.

'You must pay me off!' I shouted. 'Iqtiar-mama! I have your shoes. You must pay me before I give them to you. Do you understand?'

'I understand, Saadi,' Iqtiar said, in his bare feet. Behind him, his brothers and uncles gathered, giggling. Iqtiar was keeping a straight face. But I knew he was not cross. I knew he was expecting exactly this exchange. 'How much do you want for my shoes?'

Pultoo had told me what to ask. 'I want a thousand taka!' I said. 'Not one taka less. One thousand taka.'

'Oh, that is nonsense,' Iqtiar said. 'For one thousand taka I can buy two hundred shoes, better than those old things. I will give you twenty taka, and that is my final offer.'

'No! No! No!' I shouted. Behind me, my brother and sisters, my aunts and cousins, all Nadira's relatives, were laughing and pointing.

'I knew you shouldn't have thrown paint over Saadi,' Pultoo called. 'He is going to drive a hard bargain.'

'Twenty taka!'

'No!' I shouted.

'Thirty!'

'No!'

'Forty!'

'No, no, no, no, no!'

'He's good, this little one,' someone murmured behind me.

'Fifty!' Iqtiar said, with an air of finality.

'No!' I said. 'No, no, no, no, no. One thousand taka, or nothing!'

'Come on, Saadi,' Pultoo said, poking me in the back. In fact, he had agreed that I would refuse to take any money until Iqtiar reached fifty taka, and then I would give way and take the money. That would be mine. In the event, I was quite delirious with the excitement of standing firm in the negotiation. I saw no reason to stop at fifty. It did not occur to me that the whole business had been squared with Iqtiar.

'Very well then,' Iqtiar said. He folded his arms. He glowered down at me. He turned to his supporters, bewailing this tiny monster. 'What can I do?' he said. 'How can a man negotiate with a monster, a terror, a pocket financial genius, a merchant-king three feet tall? How is it possible? Very well then,' Iqtiar-uncle said. 'Sixty.'

From behind, Pultoo or somebody else gave me a firm shake about the head. That was good enough. Iqtiar handed over the sixty taka to me as everyone cheered and applauded and laughed. As the money went into my palm, the left shoe was taken away from me, and the right from Shibli, and Iqtiar slipped them on his bare feet. Around us, in the foyer of the hotel, people who were not invited, passers-by, complete strangers, applauded. The whole hotel glittered with light and flowers, flame and mirrors. Proceeding into the hall where the marriage was to take place, I felt at the centre of the marvellous event. It was time for Iqtiar to get married.

10.

The Kazi was inside; he was somebody that Nana knew. In a beautiful black sherwani and cap, he sat and waited patiently, smiling. I knew he had published books about religion; it was an honour, Mother had said, that he was conducting Nadira's wedding for her, and I should take care not to misbehave in front of him. He had seen the chaos of the shoe-theft before, many times, and he smiled as both sides came laughing into the room to take their places. There were two assistants with him. One was carrying a marriage register, for official purposes; the other, the Mulavi, had nothing with him. He carried what he needed in his head.

There were some official transactions to be got through. The Kazi went to Nadira, and asked her what she thought; he went to Iqtiar, now flushed but shod, and asked him the same. But you know what a wedding is like. You have seen how the veil is draped over the pair of them, a mirror before them; you know how the groom looks in the mirror and says what he feels on first seeing his bride; you know that he usually says that it is as if he has seen the moon. The Mulavi stood, and he said what he had to say: 'Enter the garden, you and your wives,' he said, his tone ringing out in the room, 'in beauty and rejoicing.' You could not help seeing how very thin the Mulavi was. His eyes were enormous in his face.

11.

Nana rose when he saw my father at the reception, and came towards him. For the first time since Nadira's wedding had begun, they embraced. Nana had chosen his moment: he wanted to embrace my father in front of everybody. The reception was held at Iqtiar's family house. They were English teachers, and their house was in the English colony in Dacca. Behind high walls, the events in the street that we had seen on driving from the wedding to the reception retreated a little bit.

'Look,' Mrs Khandekar said, to one of her friends. 'Look, my old friend is making it up with his son-in-law.'

'Making it up?' she said. 'How?'

'They fell out. There was a terrible falling-out, not between those two, but between brothers-in-law. Or so I believe. They were dividing a house between them, and some people are not made to divide a single house. It was terrible at the time, and I don't believe they have spoken for two years.'

'But it was not those two who fell out, was it?' the friend said. 'If he fell out with his brother-in-law, shouldn't he make it up with that brother-in-law?'

'I don't know that that will happen,' Mrs Khandekar said. 'But there we are.'

On a dais at the far end of the room, music began. It was a small group; players on harmonium, tabla and sitar. They sat cross-legged against fat red cushions, concentrating on their work. I did not recognize what they were playing – it was a wedding song, I now assume, so I would not have heard it before. But I recognized them. Two out of the three of them were Nadira's music teachers. There was the tall one and the short one; they were the ones Nana's family treated with such respect, standing up and saying farewell when they left for the day. On the dais, Altaf and Amit practised their art; the tabla pattered like rain, in gusts and spurts; the harmonium gave its thoughtful song; and the sitar reflectively punctuated the sound, like drops of water in a still pond. I ran up to the dais, knowing who they were, expecting that they would greet me. But they continued to play on the dais, which was draped in blue velvet. Only the harmonium player raised his face and looked at me. He smiled – he nearly smiled.

Nana was leading my father and mother up to the top table. 'Look, look,' Mrs Khandekar said. She always enjoyed a dramatic scene, and Nana making a place of special dignity for my mother and father was satisfying all her longings in this respect. But then there was a flurry of attention from the other end of the room, and people could be seen to be backing away, to be making room, to be standing if they had been sitting, and reversing if they had been standing. Nana abandoned my mother and father where they were. Who was it? Some dignitary, some judge, some painter, some poet, some film-maker, some professor, some politician? Something was drawing Nana away from the scene, but what it was nobody could tell through the crush. Somewhere in there, somebody was sparing time from his office, his fame, his celebrity, congratulating Nadira and Iqtiar, finding a kind word for Pultoo, shaking the hands of his colleagues and acquaintances. Nana hurried over, knowing his obligations.

'You will always remember today, won't you?' an old woman said to me. I could tell she was trying to be good with children. But I was more interested in the food, which was now arriving. Bowls of rice, of meat in a rich sauce, of whole fish beautifully decorated and roasted, plates of pickles, more meat, and then the vegetables: potol piled high, okra, potato and cauliflower dishes, yellow like a meadow flower, biriani, stews, curries, plates of dry grilled meat, everything you could imagine. My mother and father were seated at the best table – I could see that my mother was flushed with embarrassment and pleasure. My father, upright, was embarrassed and pleased in a different way. And it now seemed as if the drama of the scene had hardly begun. Nana's obeisance before his daughter and son-in-law, the interruption of the arriving dignitary, those had merely been prefatory to the large drama of reconciliation playing itself out at Nadira's wedding. Then, all of a sudden, there was Boro-mama, coming towards them. Mother and Father had not seen him. 'Look,' I said to Sunchita, but she had already seen him, and was saying the same thing to Sushmita. 'Look . . .'

Boro-mama took a dish of rice from one waiter, and made a gesture to another, bearing a dish of meat, to stand by him. He came to stand behind my mother and father, and I could see him saying something, quite gently. I found my hand being taken, and I looked up. It was Sharmin-aunty, wearing a vivid silver sari. On the top table, Father looked about in surprise; but on his face was an expression of pleasure and relief. Boro-mama did something very beautiful: he served my father rice, just as a waiter would, and then my mother. He handed the bowl of rice back to the waiter, and then served them both, first my father, then my mother, with the meat. He had the air of someone so unconscious of his stance, so natural in his gesture, that I did not realize almost everyone in the room was watching what he was doing. My father stood up and embraced Boro-mama. He was not an embracing man, my father, but he knew when an embrace was called for. And then I knew that everyone in the room had been watching, because the near-silence that had fallen was now broken, and everyone started talking again.

12.

Nadira-aunty and her new husband left Dacca two days later. I had never been to Dacca airport before. Perhaps I was so excited at the prospect of going there that I did not fully understand that I would never see Nadira-aunty again. This time I would get to see an aeroplane up close.

I did not know how far Sheffield was from Dacca. I knew only that it was near London, which I had seen in pictures in Nana's album. I had also seen pictures of England in a school book, from which my sisters learnt English. It was called *The Radiant Way*, and its heroes, Sushmita had told me, pointing to the pictures, were Jack and Matt, boys in ties and shorts.

I had heard stories about planes from my friend Rashid. He had an uncle named Younus, who lived and worked in Dubai. Neither Rashid nor I knew where Dubai was, nor had we seen any photograph. But many presents had come for Rashid from Dubai, carried on aeroplanes. Two-in-one tape recorders, walkie-talkie phones, tiger-faced kombol, golden tablecloths and dried dates: all these had come from Dubai, carried by Rashid's Younus-mama on an aeroplane. One day, Rashid came to my house with a toy gun. He owned up that he did not care for it and its terrible noise. He much preferred the wooden pistol he had, like mine.

Another time, Rashid's Younus-mama presented his family with a large jar of water. Rashid told me it was holy water, from Mecca. I was awestruck, and afterwards asked my mother what holy water was.

She said, 'Rubbish. Who said it was holy water?'

'Rashid,' I said.

'Well,' she said, 'if Rashid gives you any, don't drink it.'

Rashid was a boy who liked to boast, and he also showed me chocolates that had been handed out on the aeroplane to his uncle, and a pen bearing a picture of the plane. Rashid said it was the same plane that he himself had seen. Though nobody, Rashid said, could go near the plane, he had gone near it, gone with his father.

'How could they let you near the plane?' I asked.

Not only did Rashid have an uncle who travelled to Dubai, he also had a relation who worked at Dacca airport – a military official. 'He took us,' Rashid said airily.

I was eaten up with envy and longing. I wanted to see if it was the same plane that was depicted on the pen. I longed to see the plane. But mostly I longed to possess the pen with a picture of the plane on it.

'Can I come to see the planes with you?' I had said.

'My father says you need to have a big man to be allowed to go in,' Rashid said. 'Do you have an uncle in the military, by any chance?'

He knew the answer. 'No,' I said.

'I don't think you can go,' Rashid said. 'I believe you need a big man as an uncle to be allowed to go inside, to go close to the plane.'

'Acha,' I said, agreeing coldly. I did not want to discuss this any longer. I was sad, and ashamed to be sad, that I did not have any uncle who was in the military.

But now I was going to see the planes, without the help of any big man as my uncle. I was going to see them because

Nadira-aunty was going away. We went to Nana's house, and there, upstairs, Nadira was finishing her packing. There were three big brown leather suitcases.

I knew that Nadira had bought many new clothes. She was wearing a new dark blue sari – my favourite colour for her to wear – and I reached out and touched the hem. 'You like this colour on me, Saadi?' she said. 'You like this navy blue?'

I nodded. I did not know why the colour was called 'navy blue'. But Nadira always looked at her most beautiful when she wore this colour. I did not understand why. When I wore shorts of dark blue, I did not like the way it made my legs look very dark. I preferred to wear white or grey shorts, or sometimes even red. But that was my personal preference.

Nadira was placing books in the suitcase to take with her. I recognized a collection of songs by Tagore. I had seen it many times on top of the harmonium. In it was a song I loved, a song called 'We Are All Kings'; it was the only song that Nadira-aunty ever let me sing with her.

'Are you taking the harmonium?' I asked Nadira.

'No,' she said. 'It is too heavy.'

'Iqtiar-mama says he is going to buy a new one for you, Nadira,' my mother said, referring to Nadira's new husband. 'I heard him say so last night.'

'Oh, I know,' Nadira said. 'He is so sweet. But all the same . . .'

'You can't help wanting to take your own harmonium,' Nani said. 'I understand.'

And that meant a lot to Nani, since the harmonium had been given to Nadira as a present by Nana, quite out of the blue, on her sixteenth birthday.

'Well,' Nadira said, 'what is done is done. I can't take everything, and Iqtiar is going to buy me a new harmonium when we get to Sheffield. It won't be the same, but the harmoniums in England might be good in their own way.'

'And perhaps someone will be going to England, before too long,' Nani said. 'If they do, they can bring something with them.'

'Oh, Ma,' Nadira said. 'If they come . . .'

'I don't know who is coming,' Nani said.

'And perhaps no one will come,' my mother sensibly said. 'Don't take that for granted.'

'But if they do,' Nadira said, 'they could bring my notebooks, they could bring my music – they could even bring my harmonium. Who is going to England?'

'Well, it could be Omar-uncle,' my mother said. (Omar was a remote uncle; he, too, was studying in England, and flitting to and fro like a bat; he had friends studying in England; their wives, too, came and went. It could be anyone who had a spare suitcase for everything Nadira could not take with her.) But then I had a bright idea.

'Pumpkin-aunty,' I said, 'can I keep your notebooks safe?'

'Don't call me "Pumpkin",' Nadira said. 'It is not polite. I know I am fatter than I was a month ago. It is not my fault. There was just so much to eat in the last month. People would be offended if you didn't eat.'

'Pumpkin-aunty,' I said again.

'Shiri, curb your child,' Nadira said, but I pressed on.

'I'll keep your notebooks,' I said. 'I will keep them safe with my exercise books. They would never be lost there. I promise I won't lose them.'

Nadira was not cross with me for calling her 'Pumpkin'. She rubbed the back of her hand against my cheek; she would not pinch it as some grown-ups did. She gave me the most beautiful smile, and said, 'Are you sure, Little-pumpkin?'

'I promise,' I said.

'Then here you are,' Nadira said. 'They are yours. I trust you.'

The next day, we returned from the airport to our own house. By now Nadira would be in mid-air, with her clever, handsome husband. She would be above the clouds, high in the sky. This time tomorrow she would be in a completely different country, and she would be walking through it, cold and wet, but glowing in her beautiful navy blue sari. I could see her, as if in the illustrations to my English book. I went to my room, and to the shelf where my mother had placed all Nadira's notebooks. Into them she had copied her favourite songs. The first in the book was 'Amra Sobai Raja'. I smiled and held that notebook with one hand. I loved that song, 'We Are All Kings'. I started humming it. 'Amra Sobai Raja'.

13: What Happened to Them All?

1.

What happened to them?

After Nana died, the house in Dhanmondi was divided among his children. There was a lawsuit, which I am not going to go into. Boro-mama threw himself at the legal questions with all the energy he was capable of. It went on for some years, creating a good deal of bad blood. At the end of it, the house and its plot were divided between three – Boro-mama, Choto-mama and my mother. (The aunts were satisfied to take possession of some other property in the north of Dacca and in the country-side that my grandfather had been amassing over the years.) Boro-mama took over most of the land that went with the Dhanmondi house, and moved his family into the servants' house in the garden. He did not enjoy it for very long. As often happens at the end of very long lawsuits, he died, quite suddenly, a month after its conclusion. His wife and children quickly sold the land to developers, as most of Dhanmondi was doing in the 1990s. Choto-mama and my mother divided the house, deprived of most of its land, between them, and did not sell it. Nowadays, half the house is lived in by my brother, his wife and children; the other half is Pultoo's – he has a painting academy where my grandfather's law library used to be. The last time I was in Dacca, the mothers of the district kept coming in with their shy and delighted children, each of them with a paintbox and a portfolio, and the sun shone through the leaves of the tamarind and mango trees, still just as they were in the front garden.

The end Sheikh Mujib came to is known to everyone. They were not so very far from us, so we heard the noise of his end, too. You will find in the history books the reason why some people were so very angry with him. I just remember being woken up, very early on an August morning, by the noise of demolition, the crackle, once more, of fire and gunshot. It was very close indeed. By then everybody knew what to do when this happened. My mother got us up and bustled us, still clutching our coverlets, into the salon, away from the road, far from any public windows. My father telephoned a friend, a government official who lived nearby – it was only six in the morning, but people in those days slept on their nerves, and woke quickly at the sound of gunfire. The friend said only this: 'It's happened.'

Somewhere around five in the morning, a tank was driven through the front wall of Sheikh Mujib's house. Military officers entered the house. Sheikh Mujib did not live with much security. He had gone on walking to Sufiya's all through his presidency. He must have had guns in the house, but that was all. All his family were there, apart from two daughters. One of those was Sheikh Hasina, the daughter who had so amused my mother with her meanness over a few sacks of chilli: she was in Germany. Sheikh Mujib's sons and their wives and children, his wife and other family members were roused immediately. We know that the wives took their children to Sheikh Mujib's wife's bedroom as fast as they could. Perhaps they thought that there might be safety there. Or perhaps they wanted to die together. The soldiers shot them all. An adult son of Sheikh Mujib's fled into his bath-room, where the killers found him, breaking down the door and shooting into the room, smashing the glass on the wall. Sheikh Mujib went to meet his murderers on the stairs. He was a very simple man, and said, 'What do you want?' to them. They are said to have spoken a brief arraignment, although this informa-tion only comes from them, years later, in the cause of their own propaganda and defence. They may, in reality, have shot straight away, killing Sheikh Mujib on the stairs of his own house. For many years, he had been known by his honorific title of Bangobandhu, a title awarded him by the students in the late 1960s: a Friend of Bengal. Nobody survived.

The house was not demolished afterwards, but simply shut up and abandoned. In later years, it was reopened as a museum, just as it had been left on that August morning when my father's friend said, 'It's happened,' to him over the telephone. Sheikh Mujib's bedroom toiletries are exactly where they were, showing that his preferred brand of talcum was Johnson's baby powder, and that, like most sophisticated men in the world at that particular time, his habitual cologne was the beautiful oriental scent, Old Spice. These remain on his dressing-table; also undisturbed are the shattered mirror in his son's bathroom, his blood on the stairs, preserved by Perspex sheets, and, dried on to the ceiling of his wife's bedroom, fragments of the brains of his daughters-in-law and grandchildren. You may visit the museum where the Friend of Bengal lived and died in Dhanmondi six days a week, between ten a.m. and five p.m.

'He was a very simple man,' Sufiya's daughter Sultana will tell you. 'Once, when I was very young, and of no purpose or use to anyone, I was very late for my class at the university, and Sheikh Mujib's big black sedan drew up as I was hurrying along. He was not yet president of the country, but still, everyone in the country knew who he was. He popped his head out of the window and said, "Can I give you a lift?" Just as the daughter of his old friend, you understand. Well, I demurred, and he insisted, and so I got in, wondering how it would look when I was dropped off for my class at the university by Sheikh Mujib – you know how these things worry you when you are young. But he chatted away quite happily, about Hasina his daughter, who was in my class, of course, and asking how we all were, and before I knew it, we were at the courthouse. He apologized greatly, very simply, very sincerely, but he said he would have to get out before me. His driver would take me wherever I wanted to go, but he had to get out here, at the courthouse. "You see," he said, "they want to send me to jail again." You know, at this time, he was always being sent off to jail by the Pakistanis. "And I really must be on time to be prosecuted. If I am late, they are only going to send me to jail again for contempt of court, the scoundrels." That is what he said. So he got out at the courthouse, and I had the very great embarrassment of drawing up at the university in this great black car, and everyone thinking it was my family's car. I believe that Sheikh Mujib was as embarrassed by this splendour as I was. He had a nice sense of humour. He may have wanted me to know just how embarrassing it was to be driven about in this way.'

Sheikh Mujib himself was buried in his village, but the twenty members of his family and household who were killed on that August morning are buried together, in a line of sad, noble hummocks, in the cemetery in Dacca – Dhaka, the city is now called. The men who killed them afterwards became Members of Parliament, ministers, ambassadors; only many years later, three and a half decades, were they brought to trial for their crimes. The victims for whose death they were tried, and go on being tried, included the eight-year-old Sheikh Russell, who died pleading to be sent abroad to his sister in Germany, and two unborn children.

I went to see Sufiya in her beautiful house when she was very old. The house was just as it had been: people still came to visit her, to drink tea, to interest her in radical causes. Sometimes, she said, the people who came to see her did so out of mindless curiosity, and some of them even stole a book as a memento from the bookshelf on the terrace. 'Everyone thinks I am a rich woman and can afford to replace anything,' she complained mildly. 'But I am not. And in any case, books are like people. You cannot replace them. I wish people would understand that.' She had survived the announcement of her death on Calcutta radio by decades. By her extreme old age, the house she lived in was no longer surrounded by other houses: her neighbours had sold their land to developers, and all about her blocks of luxury flats had risen. In Dhanmondi, her house remained, its garden in the perpetual near darkness imposed on it by high-rises; Sheikh Mujib's house remained, turned into a museum; and my grandfather's house remained, just as it was. There were not many others. I felt this was a bond between me and Sufiya, and I went to see her to ask her to speak at a rally for the Burmese politician Aung San Suu Kyi. She received me very courteously; she gave me a cup of tea with sandesh and samosas; she said she would write a letter in support, but she was, alas, too old to leave the house to give a speech at the rally, as I asked. She did write a letter, a beautiful one, which the leader of the student movement read out at the rally, and that was the last time I saw her.

She died, full of honours, of nothing worse than old age; the state gave her a funeral, and many tens of thousands of people came. The offer was made to lay her in the field in front of the parliament building, that lovely grey fort by an American architect, begun by the Pakistanis, finished by the Bangladeshis. But she said she would prefer to be in the ordinary cemetery with everyone else. She liked other people, and I think she would have felt lonely in the field of honour with nobody but a president or two to keep her company. I have been told that almost her last words, in the hospice where she died, were 'Has Tulsi eaten properly?'

Tulsi was the nurse who had been assigned to look after her in her last days.

2.

Many years later, I married a writer, who has listened to the story as I have told it to him. One of his books was translated into Romanian, and he was required to travel to that country, with the strange white palace, the largest in the world, at its useless centre. While he was there, he told me, he had dinner with his Romanian publisher and the publisher's wife. The publisher's wife was, it seemed, a well-known journalist in Romania, and many years before, she had been sent by the Romanian Bureau of Overseas Journalism to cover the conflict in East Pakistan. She had not thought – she said, lighting another cigarette over a half-full plate in the restaurant – she had not thought that she would be covering the birth of a new nation. She had not known that new nations were born in such a way. She had imagined, she said, that she would be covering the repression of a revolt, and the resumption of ordinary life under the previous political masters.

(I guess that she started telling this story because my husband explained who I was, and where I came from, and what stories about me he could remember, and dull things like that. He spared my feelings. He did not tell me so.)

But there, one day, was a new nation. No one knew what had

happened to its new leader: Sheikh Mujib – the man whom Nana, and Khandekar, and Sultana had known and been neighbours to – was in prison in Pakistan, and would not be released for months. There did not seem much hope for the new country, if there was a new country. But the Pakistanis had left in mud and blood and smoke, leaving nothing much but informers behind them in their borrowed houses.

The publisher's wife had left her hotel and walked towards the centre of Dacca, to see what there was to be seen. She had needed, after all, a story to write. There was nothing. Nobody was about at all. People had not heard. (This is what she said, though I have seen the newspaper of the first day of the new country many times since, and I think she was not quite correct in her memory.) They would, she assumed, come out of their houses in time. They preferred not to be the first one on the street. The first one on the street was, in fact, the Romanian publisher's wife, who had no fear, and who trod the tank-torn highway with interest, listening for signs of life.

There was no sound, she said. A silence, which is unusual in Dacca; there were fewer cars and lorries in Dacca in 1971, but there were some, and there would always be the noises of the street. It was so quiet that she could hear the birds singing. She had no idea there were birds left alive to sing in the centre of Dacca. She had been walking for nearly ten minutes in this silent city when a sound drew her attention from a nearby quarter, a street or two into the warren. For one second she thought it must be the noise of a machine-gun, far off, but it was close and quiet and mechanical. She identified it: it was the sound of a sewing-machine, hard at work.

She made her way into the back-streets, and after a couple of turns, there was a tailor, sitting under the awning of his shop, his Panjabi shirt flapping as he worked the pedals of his old British sewing-machine. He smiled enormously, nodding as he fed what he was working under the needle. 'I could not imagine what it was,' the Romanian publisher's wife said, retelling the story. 'Then

305

I saw – it was a flag. It was the flag you saw at demonstrations, but here it was, the flag of the new country, and he was making it as best he could. It is hard, you know, to cut out a circle accurately, but he had done quite a good job of making a red circle, and he had sewn it properly on his green flag, his green rectangle, you know, a little to the right of centre. He explained it all to me, as if I had never heard it before – the red was the blood shed in the struggle for independence, and the green . . . ah, I forget what the green was for. He finished it. I asked him what he was going to do now, and do you know what he said? He said, "I'm going to make another one." He spoke quite good English, and I complimented him on it. His father had made suits in Calcutta, for Englishmen. But that day he was only going to make flags, until he ran out of the cloth he had dyed himself. So I asked him if I could buy one, on this special day, and he sold it to me for, I think, two dollars.' She had folded up the flag, and taken it home to Romania, and had kept it ever since.

Two years after that, her journalistic privileges of travel were revoked, and for twenty years, she never again left her country, and had never been back to mine. That was what my husband's Romanian publisher told him, and I think she believed it, having told it many times, though the streets of Dacca were certainly not empty on the morning of independence, but crowded with celebrants, letting off firecrackers. Still, that was the story as she told it, and the story she liked to tell, so I have told it too, however untruthfully.

This has been the story of my early life. I have tried not to invent anything, and to tell everything as I was told it. I have tried to be as good a storyteller as my mother was. In later years, my mother's girlhood acquaintance Sheikh Hasina came to be prime minister of the country. She was Sheikh Mujib's daughter. My mother would sometimes say, 'Was it Hasina who liked that dish that Sharmin used to cook – you remember, the way she steamed rui with ginger and lemon? Do you remember? I know we used to cook it when we were all living in Papa's house, all through that summer. Don't you remember? It was so simple, but very good. We never tired of it, remember? And afterwards I'm sure that Hasina came to dinner once at somebody's house, and they'd had Sharmin's rui recipe, and so they asked us for the recipe to cook for Hasina, and Hasina liked it so much we gave the recipe to her as well, and she said she would always cook rui like that in future. I'm almost sure. I can't think who it was who was having Hasina round for dinner. Could it have been Kamal? I really can't think. Of course, Hasina has always been peculiar about food. I remember, when we were both girls, I went round to their house with Sultana, and she was in a fury. It was for no reason at all. You see, she had ordered up thirteen sacks of chillis from the country. Was it thirteen sacks? I'm almost sure it was. But what would Hasina be doing with thirteen sacks of chillis? And when the sacks had arrived, the very morning that Sultana and I were visiting her, she had gone to the kitchen to count them, and there were only eleven. A whole two sacks had gone missing on the way. Imagine. You see . . .'

And my father would tuck his napkin into his collar in his dry way. He would cough reprovingly at this point in the story, and smile at my mother to show that he was not serious. He would say, 'Not Hasina and her sacks of chillis again. We must have heard this story so many times.'

London-Geneva-Dhaka
January 2011

Author's Note

This is a novel of the formation of Bangladesh. Until 1971, it formed an eastern province of Pakistan, divided from the western part by geography, language, and culture. It broke from the western side in a savagely violent war of independence. In December 1971, after the deaths of uncounted innocent victims in the civil war, a new country was declared: Bangla Desh, the Home of the Bengalis.

Scenes from Early Life is the story of one upper-middle-class Bengali family, a novel which is told in the form of a memoir. The narrator speaks in the voice of Zaved Mahmood, the author's husband, who was born in late 1970 shortly before the outbreak of the war of independence.

Acknowledgements

A word about names. All Bengalis have a proper, formal name which they often acquire when they first go to school, or on another early encounter with officialdom. These are not much used in this story. Then most of them have a pet name, used by family and close friends – this is the way in which most of the characters are referred to here. Bengalis are much more ready than Europeans to refer to their relations by the degree of the relationship. Here, the ones most commonly used are *mama* and *mami*, meaning (maternal) uncle and aunt, *nana* and *nani*, meaning (maternal) grandparents, *bhai*, brother, and *appa*, sister. Where necessary, these are qualified by *boro*, meaning big, or *choto*, meaning small. Hence the narrator's two maternal uncles are referred to as Boro-mama, Big-uncle, or Laddu, and the younger as Choto-mama, Small-uncle, or Pultoo. That is what their family tends to call them, although neither is a formal name that would be entered on a government form.

Mujibur Rahman, the first president of Bangladesh, was much more frequently referred to as Sheikh Mujib, which is the name I have preferred to use, but also by the splendid honorific Bango-bandhu, the Friend of Bengal, a name you will still hear on Bangladeshi lips. I have reserved this for very elevated circumstances, although for many Bangladeshis it seems quite ordinary.

This is not a history of the struggle for Bangladesh's independence, but the rendering of a family's passionately held memories. It does not pretend to be an account of the millions who died in the war and the famines that followed. These are the emphases of my husband's memories, and they may coincide with others' or flatly contradict them. But in any case, this is not the full story, which could never be told.

I would like to thank the many friends and family in Bangladesh who welcomed me into their houses and shared their memories of this time. Sultana and Sayeeda Kamal invited me into the beautiful house of their mother, Begum Sufiya Kamal, and shared memories of her and of Zainul Abedin, showing me many treasures. The house in Dhanmondi still stands, alone where all its neighbours have been replaced by high-rises, and I would like to thank its current occupants, Syed Hasan Mahmud (Choto-mama) and my brother-in-law Zahid for their welcome. Also miraculously preserved in a fast-developing city is the house in Rankin Street, along with its neighbour; Mr A. R. Khan welcomed us in, and shared his vivid memories of the time of Zaved's childhood. I would also like to thank the Hossain family, especially Sara Hossain and David Bergman, Mr Helal of the Bangladeshi Parliament, for sparing time from his crowded schedule to show me around Louis Kahn's wonderful building, Farah Ghuznavi for her hospitality at her family's enchanted *rajbari*, and many other friends in Bangladesh and elsewhere. Particular thanks go to my poet brother-in-law Jahir Hasan for generously finding me translations of several important and near-unobtainable classics from the mainstream of the Bengali literary arts, including Shahidullah Kaiser's *Sangshaptak*, the work of one of the intellectuals targeted and murdered by Pakistani forces in the course of the genocide. A deep debt of literary gratitude is acknowledged in the last sentence of the novel.

As is clear, this account, with its gaps and wilfully ahistorical emphases, has not been shaped by systematic research. But among the books I found most useful and helpful in complementing my vivid interlocutors were Jahanara Imam's diary of her 1971 experiences, the harrowing and passionate *Of Blood and Fire*, and Archer K. Blood's outsider's account, *The Cruel Birth of Bangladesh* (both the University Press, Dhaka).